a girl named Josie

a novel

KARA JEFFERIES

Six Dogs Publications
PO box 407
Prosper, Texas 75078
www.SixDogsPublishing.com
www.karajefferies.com

ISBN 979-8-9896430-8-0 Softcover
ISBN 979-8-9896430-9-7 Digital online

Publisher's Cataloging-In-Publication Data
(Prepared by Cassidy's Cataloguing Services)

Design by Vanessa Mendozzi
Edited by Sarah Ridding and Sara Oestreich

Printed in the United States of America

To the girls who were led to believe they were never enough, who faced rejection and feared heartbreak, and who wore a brave smile despite the pain inside—this book is for you. May you find strength, hope, and the knowledge that you are truly worthy.

Prologue

My phone rings, and the name on my screen makes me freeze. "Shit," I say under my breath; my heart is thundering in my chest and I don't know what to do. I can't avoid her forever, but I didn't think she'd call so soon. I saved her number to my contacts so she couldn't catch me off guard. But she's still managed to tip my world off its axis.

I wouldn't say I like confrontation. I avoid it at all costs, but the girl on the other end of this phone would starve without it. She's direct and makes no effort to be warm or friendly. But despite her reserved demeanor, her beauty is undeniable. Every head in the room turns in her direction when she enters. She's everything a girl would want to be.

A voicemail alert appears on my home screen; I hit play and put the phone up to my ear.

"What the fuck, Joy? You can't keep him from me, and why would you even make him choose? I don't care what is happening with you, but your insecurities are not my problem. Stop dodging me and call me back."

"Okay," I say out loud. "That was interesting." Oh God, what if she comes to my apartment? I can't avoid her forever.

She growls in frustration before she hangs up. Immediately a text pops up:

Oh, and everyone says your personality is indicative of your name. I'm calling bullshit, Joy. You're a broken mess just like the rest of us. YOU WON'T WIN.

Chapter 1

My grandma left everything she owned to me, which only exaggerated the tension between my mom and me. For my mom, the hurt was twofold. First, my grandma took me in as a child and raised me when my mom didn't want to. Second, leaving me everything was my grandmother's final act to ensure I was taken care of, so I wouldn't need any help from my mom or from anyone for that matter, even as an adult.

I intended to use her money to buy a house, but a week before closing, I canceled the contract. Running away from big decisions is a habit I may not be able to break.

I had the opportunity to receive a full-ride scholarship to play soccer at a college up in northern California, but I turned it down. What's even worse than turning it down is the reason behind my decision—a guy, of course. I wish I could say he was the one who got away, but he wasn't; he was the one who got me pregnant and then ran away. Now, it's me who's running again, running from another commitment. I only put an offer on that house because that's what everyone expected me to do. Managing others' exceptions is all I know. Kids like me have to base our decisions on pleasing those around us. We can't disobey or test boundaries; if we do, we could end up without anywhere to sleep. Buying a house with money left to me was the responsible thing to do, but as the date got closer, I realized my grandma didn't leave me that money to tie me down. She left it to me to set me free. So, that has been my philosophy ever since: not to get tied down.

My phone rings in my hand, and the caller ID reads: *My Fave.*

"Hey!" I answer.

"Meet me for a run?" Roxanne's quiet voice comes through the phone.

"Is that a demand or a request?"

"Both. You know where to meet."

"Okay, it'll take me about ten minutes to get there," I concede because it's Roxy, and she doesn't take no for an answer.

Roxanne and I have been best friends for at least fifteen years. We played soccer together growing up (well, more against each other), we run together, and we work together. Which technically makes her a co-worker, but friends first.

When I get to our meeting spot, Roxy has been waiting for me for a minute because her breathing isn't labored at all.

"How long are we running today?" I ask, already out of breath since she beat me here. She had an opportunity to catch her breath, and well, obviously, I didn't.

"Let's do five miles," she says, her long, brown ponytail bouncing from left to right.

"Is that including the half mile I ran to get to you and the half mile I'll run once we separate?" I whine.

"Stop it… Let's go." She takes off in a full sprint.

"Hey," I shout. "Wait up. Did you see my Instagram post last night? It was pretty good?"

"Are you sure you're okay?" she questions.

I live in a great apartment on the third floor, not far from work. My west-facing balcony gives me a front-row seat to the most amazing sunsets. I post sunset pictures almost every night, and they're taking over my social media footprint, which is depressing and, I'm assuming, the basis for her question.

"I'm fine," I insist.

"Are you sure because you haven't been on a second date since you and Gabe broke up?"

"And?" I question because one-word answers and replies are all I can manage with our current pace.

"*And* you need to give guys a chance, a second date. Your philosophy of not being tied down is exhausting at this point."

"How long have you been holding that one in?" I ask, giving her a side-eye.

"Come on, Joy, I'm on your side. It's been several months since you and Gabe broke things off; you need to put yourself out there again."

Gabe and I dated for about six months. We weren't exclusive, and we both had different reasons for not committing. His reason was that I'd never be his forever, and mine was that no one had ever wanted me, and I was afraid of committing to someone and getting my heart broken.

"Earth to Joy," Roxy says. "Where did you go to?"

"Can we walk for the last half-mile? I think I may die," I say as I lean forward with my hands on my knees, trying to catch my breath so I can explain myself to Roxy.

"Listen, Rox. I'm not mad at Gabe, and I'm not avoiding guys, but the guys you and Chris keep setting me up with are unattractive and boring. I'm sorry. It's just that Chris's standards are very different from mine."

Chris, or Christopher, is Roxanne's boyfriend. He's older than us by ten years and much different than anyone she's ever dated, and his friends are much different than any guy she's ever dated. I'm drawn to your stereotypical tall, dark, and handsome – the type not searching for Ms. Right, but rather Ms. Right Now. I'm not looking for love, just someone to have fun with. However, Chris's friends are fixated on settling down, with conversation always leading to marriage and children. I've never been asked about my five-year plan more than when I am on a date with one of his friends.

"Gabe was honest from day one, and I was tired of replacing batteries in my boyfriend."

We laugh as I try to keep her pace. Even walking with this girl kills me.

"I feel like you've buried yourself in work since you and Gabe broke-up."

"I have," I answer. "But only because I'm bored."

I'm a sales manager at a dealership. I don't love the job, but I do love the money. The schedule sucks too, but when you don't have a social life, does working a shitty work schedule matter? All the family guys hate it because they miss Saturday baseball, soccer, basketball… You name it, they miss it. I try not to make that my issue, but being the people pleaser I am, I often switch a weekday shift for a weekend, but not without a coffee or free lunch. I mean, I'm not a total pushover.

I know how it feels not to have anyone cheering you on at a game, and if I can save one child from feeling what I felt, I will.

"I just want to ensure the guys aren't exploiting your generosity."

"Rox, all my decisions are intentional these days. If I want a Saturday off, I'll take it, but when you don't have kids and only have work, what is the difference between a Saturday and a Tuesday—just a name? I don't let guys at work guilt me into extra shifts; I do it because I want to."

"Okay, I just want to make sure you're looking out for yourself and not the guys at work."

"I've got it under control. I'm good."

"Did you go out with Landon from finance?" she asks, changing the subject.

"No! I told you I'm not dating anyone from the dealership."

Working in a male-dominated industry is interesting to say the least. I get hit on by not only customers but co-workers as well. One rule… DO NOT DATE COWORKERS. It never ends well.

"Look what happened to Harper. I refuse to let that happen to me," I add.

Gabe (my ex-boyfriend in question) fell for a girl at work, and everything blew up in his face. They ended up together eventually, but not before she had to transfer to a different dealership because they tortured each other for months. "I get it," Roxy says. "But not dating co-workers never made sense; a co-worker shares the same drive as you and the same education level. So, by default, isn't that a better place to find a partner than a bar?" She looks at me with a firm jaw; her eyes are locked on mine, asking for me to validate her observation.

"I don't know, but you know I don't keep guys for long. And the last thing I need is an ex-boyfriend at work. I'm just too nice, and they lose interest, and around and around we go."

Roxanne and I make it back to our meeting spot, but before we go our separate ways, she asks, "Are you getting ready for the run?"

"I already told you I'm not running a 5K, a half marathon, a full marathon, or a triathlon. That's your thing, not mine."

She moans, "Ugh, you're impossible. Call me when you make it home, and make sure you run the rest of the way since we walked a mile."

"You're mean," I yell over my shoulder as I run the last half mile home.

In my free time, I run, and it brings me peace. Being outside running with AirPods makes me feel everything and nothing simultaneously. Some days, I'm fully committed to the run, determined to beat my last best time—music loud in my ears, nothing in my head but the hill in front of me. Arms tight to my body, one foot in front of the other until the run ends. No quitting, no slowing down, mind over matter. Then there are days I can't keep a steady pace to save my life. My mind wanders to all the corners of the world. What needs to be done at work? What needs to be cleaned at home? Remember your grandma, don't let a day go by without thinking of her and what she did for you.

My favorite run days are when the weather is perfect, and I can hear the fountains over my music, and it's breathtaking enough to make me stop and appreciate the world around me.

Three minutes into the final stretch home, my AirPods alert me that I have a new text from Roxanne. I run with a backpack, large enough only for my phone. I usually wouldn't check my text messages, but since we just separated, I want to make sure she's okay. Trying not to slow my pace, I reach around my back to grab my phone. When that doesn't work, I unhook the front strap and bring my pack forward. Looking inside, I pull out my phone and run into what feels like a block wall. I stop immediately and try to catch my breath.

I look up and see Xavier.

"Joy, is that you?" he asks.

"Xavier?" I say, shock evident in my voice. Xavier is the cousin of Harper Atwood. Harper lived in my apartment building, and she's why my ex-boyfriend Gabe broke things off with me.

Xavier and I met and talked a few times in passing when he visited her, which was often. Xavier is a dream. He's just over six feet tall, with ocean-blue eyes and light-brown messy hair. He's muscular with olive-colored skin. Today, he is shirtless, dripping in sweat, and still looks and smells fantastic. I can see the outline of every one of his ab muscles. He's perfection. I've always noticed how cute he is, but I don't think I've ever seen how sexy this man is, probably because I've always been afraid to make eye contact when he's with Harper.

Yes, she's that bad. She could teach a course on the perfect resting bitch face. She says whatever is on her mind without thinking how it will affect others around her. I run from conflict; she runs to it like a moth to light. We couldn't be any more different. While I'm utterly lost, looking over Xavier's sculpted body, he pulls out one of my AirPods and says, "Shit, Joy, are you okay?"

I try to reply, but par for the course, I stammer and only manage to get out, "Umm yeah, I think so. Are you?"

He laughs and says, "I'm fine, but you ran into me with your head down; I was able to prepare myself for the impact."

Embarrassed, I say, "Oh yeah, I am so sorry." Stammering over my words again, I say, "My phone… and I was struggling… Ugh, never mind." I shake my head. *Get it together, Joy.* My God, I sound like a love-struck pre-teen.

He frowns, saying, "You really need to look where you're running. You can get hit by a car, and you shouldn't run with both AirPods in."

Did he just scold me? I wrinkle my nose, so he adds, "You can't hear someone coming from behind. Wearing both AirPods makes you a target."

His statement catches me off guard, but in a positive way, making me perceive him as a possessive and protective man, not just the cute guy who hangs out at my apartment building with his mean cousin.

I mean Xavier barely knows me, and he's advising me on how to stay safe.

I smile, open my eyes wide, and say, "Thank you for the advice. I never considered how dangerous wearing both AirPods could be. I had no idea kidnapping was something I needed to worry about in our small city." The whole time, suppressing a giggle.

"Joy, you're too sweet for sarcasm," he says, shaking his head.

"Oh no, I'm not being sarcastic at all. You don't think of those things until it's too late. It's never an issue until it is. I get your point, and I appreciate your concern?" The word concern comes out as a question, and we pause for a minute, making this literal run-in a thousand times more awkward than it was just seconds ago.

I look down at my watch and say, "Well, I better get going before my run app starts yelling at me like a mean gym coach. Again, thanks for the advice; I promise to keep it in mind moving forward."

He nods in agreement. "Yeah, I have to get back as well." His concern is evident by his furrowed eyebrows, creating two vertical wrinkles between them. He asks again, "Are you sure you're okay?" His expression is a mix of confusion and lingering concern, a subtle indication that he is genuine.

"Yes, I'm fine. Again, I'm so sorry for running into you. I almost feel like we should exchange insurance information."

He laughs and says, "It was good to see you, Joy."

I continue my run, but my mind is a million miles away, replaying my run-in with Xavier and how he said, *"It was good to see you"* over and over again.

Chapter 2

My cell rings as I get out of the shower still soaking wet and dripping all over my tiles. I dry off my hand and hit the speaker button, and since I move a few feet from my phone to wrap my dripping hair, I shout, "Hey," still a little short of breath from my run.

"Hey!" Roxy says. "What's wrong? Why are you out of breath?"

"I just got back from a run, and I'm dripping all over my floor," I exclaim.

"Two days in a row, I like it. How was your run?" she asks, which is a little weird for her to say because I pretty much run every day.

"It was fine," I draw out each word for dramatic effect. "Why are you being weird right now?"

"What are you doing tomorrow?"

"Why are you not answering my question and continuing your interrogation about my run?"

"I need a favor," she says.

"I knew it!" I shout, a little too proud of myself because I know my best friend too well. "What do you want from me, Roxy?"

"I need a running partner for the relay tomorrow."

"What!" I yell. "Oh, hell no! Roxanne, we literally just had this conversation yesterday. I don't do marathons. I have nothing to prove. I run for therapy, and so I can eat all the cookies I want."

"Please," she begs. "Technically, this isn't a marathon. It's a relay, and you didn't have a relay on your list yesterday."

"Semantics," I reply.

She continues, "Christopher has to work, and I already paid. Come on, it's for charity. I can't back out, and you can't deny me, or it'll be back, Karma. Some dogs need blankets for the winter, and if you don't do this, you could be responsible for some of them freezing to death."

"Seriously, drama queen," I say in my very dry tone.

"Please, I can't do this alone. It's a relay race that requires two people."

"What about one of your sisters?" I ask, already resigned to participating in the race if she can't find anyone else, yet secretly hoping for an alternative."

"Busy, working and traveling," she answers.

"Your brother?"

"Too vulgar to repeat."

"Ugh," I yell into the phone. "Why did I answer?"

"Because you love me," she says happily.

"Text me the info, pick me up, and bring me water," I say, disappointed.

"I love you so much, bestie."

"I fucking hate you, Roxy."

I end the call and immediately, my phone dings with a text. I open it to find a selfie of Roxanne showing off a perfectly white smile that stretches from ear to ear as she gives me a thumbs-up.

Roxanne has always had the best smile, one that lights up her face. And one I can never say no to. The contrast of her white teeth against her olive-colored skin and dark features seems to get her most of what she wants in life. That and her hair, which is a rich dark brown with subtle hints of red that show only in the sunlight. Her eyes, a cooler, deeper shade of brown, pair perfectly with her long black eyelashes that always capture attention. Even though she's master of getting what she wants and I'm usually to shy or awkward to be so upfront with people, our most significant difference is her tendency to stress, a trait I tease her about. She claims I don't stress enough.

My cell phone rings again the following day, and it's none other than Roxanne. I debate not answering but know she won't stop calling until I do.

"Hello," I draw out.

"Hurry up, we're going to be late!"

"Do you have everything?" I ask.

"Yes. Hurry up! Your coffee is hot and sugary, and the water is cold. Now get down here."

"Okay. Okay, I'll be down in two seconds," I groan as I pick up my purse and head to her car.

I jump in her Honda Civic with a million miles. Her personalized license plate reads FO XY01; it's cute when you're sixteen, not so much when you're twenty-four.

Without a word, we speed away from the front of my apartment building.

"Slow down, speed racer; it's a foot race, not a car race," I say, laughing.

"Just buckle up so we can get there. I don't want to be late and lost." She's antsy this morning.

"What's bothering you?" I know she's upset. We've been friends for far too long, so for her to think I can't read every emotion she wears is absurd.

"It's Christopher."

"And," I say, trying to pull out the actual story.

"He's not working today."

"Okay, it's me. Are you going to tell me, or will we play the guessing game?"

She's very uncomfortable, stares straight ahead, and drives. She sighs. "Remember how Christopher used to live with someone?"

"Yeah, wasn't her name Christy?"

Roxy glares at me from the corner of her eye and says, "That's not important, Joy."

I cringe and continue, "He's ten years older than us; it's not surprising he has been in a few serious and casual relationships before you. It's never been an issue for you, so why now?"

"Well, she's back and trying to guilt him into getting back together."

"Shit," I say. "I mean, it's Chris; he loves you. He won't go back to her."

"Maybe, but we decided to take a break yesterday. Her gaze is fixed on the road ahead, though I don't miss the glint of emptiness in her eyes.

"Oh, Rox, I'm so sorry." I mean, what do you say in this situation? I can call Chris all sorts of names, but they're going to get back together eventually, so that will bite me in the ass later. "I don't know what to say," is all that I say as I put my hand on her leg, since I can't hug her.

"You don't have to say anything. I'm fine."

"You're not fine, and that's okay. You know you don't always have to be fine."

"I know, but really, I'm fine for now. I don't think we're breaking up for good, and if we do, then we do."

"I'll never choose anyone over you, Joy," she says quietly.

"I'll never ask you to," I reply.

Chapter 3

I'm starting the race because the anxiety of waiting for my turn will make me vomit. And, with Roxy being faster than me, she can pick up any time we need toward the end of the race. Growing up, she was also a soccer player, but she's built like a soccer player. I am not. Her calves are big and defined, especially for her small stature. When she wears heels, her leg muscles are sculpted and visible. Mine are not; they're toothpicks. Short and skinny.

She runs to stay in shape like me, but she runs fast. No matter how hard I try, I can't keep up with her pace for any length of time without slowing her down. Our run the other day is a perfect example of this; I struggled to maintain our conversation while she effortlessly jogged along her ponytail, swinging back and forth and taunting me. When I suggested walking, she remained unfazed. Despite my limitations, we still run together almost every night after work.

I keep reminding her that this is for charity, not a US Olympic event. She is the most competitive person that I've ever met. When you have four siblings, you have to do something to stand out.

The train horn blows, and that's my cue to run. The first mile is the easiest today because I'm fueled by pure adrenaline. My once ten-minute mile is cut to eight minutes right now. The second mile will also be easy because that is when my body will be warmed up, and my muscles will be primed. It's miles three and four I worry about. Mile five will also be easy because of the noise from the crowd. It's unbelievable what outside influences affect your body's ability to perform. There is no better feeling than knowing that you're the reason all those people on the sideline scream your last name. A name that they would never know if it wasn't for your jersey nameplate.

I'd often allow my mind to wander during soccer games when I was growing up, similar to how it wanders when I run. When I was younger, the kind of questions that ran around my mind were: Who's watching in the crowd? What school assignments are due on Monday? Now it's: Do I have food at home to eat for dinner? What time am in work tomorrow?

AirPods in, and I just hit mile three. My pace has slowed, but I'm hoping I'm at eight and a half minutes per mile. I need to stay below nine minutes not to disappoint Roxanne. I keep thinking about how much I hate Roxanne right now and question why I let her talk me into doing things I hate. I'm not easily influenced, nor was I in high school. Honestly, I don't think anyone cared enough to influence me. I wasn't popular even though I was the best player on my team. No one ever wanted to hang out with me outside of practice, and I can't say I blame them. I wouldn't want to hang out with my high-school self, either.

By mile three and a half, my mind continues to wander. I'd have to say that's the downfall of running for me. At work, my mind is engaged; playing soccer, my mind is always on high alert, anticipating the next play. Running is second nature, and my body knows what to do without me telling it. One foot in front of the other; it's something we do as toddlers. The simple art of running doesn't take athletic ability. It takes endurance and willpower. Competition running is a whole different beast that I'm not qualified for.

As I struggle to keep my pace, my mind drifts back to the memory of how Gabe and I first met. I replay it like a meet-cute scene from a rom-com movie; it's funny, considering how much I hate doing things alone. I was alone and completely out of place at a manager's training conference. He could feel how uncomfortable I was and shamelessly introduced himself. We hit it off immediately, and from that moment on, we were inseparable, that was, until Harper went to work at his dealership. His sense of humor is probably my favorite thing about him. His introduction is one I'll never forget; he approached me with a cheeky grin and said, "Hey, I'm looking for a girl of average height with shoulder-length strawberry blonde hair. Have you seen her?"

Shaking my head in amusement, I replied, "With just five girls at this training, I'm the closest to a strawberry blonde. So, why the search for this girl? I should be in the loop since I'm helping you find her."

He responded again, wearing the same cheeky smile that highlights his dimples, "She looks completely out of her element, and if that doesn't change, the guys in this room will eat her alive. I figured we could partner up, and maybe I could buy her lunch."

"So, you're hoping to be her hero?" I counter with a very judgmental expression.

Sheepishly, he replied, "No, not a hero, just her friend."

And that's how Gabe won me over; he's funny, like I mentioned before, but he's honest and caring. We agreed to keep our relationship casual and to always be upfront with each other. He kept his end of the bargain. I don't begrudge him, but why Harper? She has never had a nice thing to say to me. She never apologized to me or even asked if I was okay. For Christ's sake, we lived in the same building, and I talked to her cousin more than her. I don't have the capacity for girls like Harper Atwood.

I hit mile four, and all I can think about is how break-ups destroy people. Why am I thinking about break-ups during a race? It's probably because it's all I ever think about. I'm not a stranger to break-ups, but I won't allow them to destroy me. They're more of an expectation at this point in my life; men never stay; maybe they leave because I'm too nice, or perhaps they go because I'm not enough. I wasn't enough for my dad, so how could I ever think I'd be enough for a stranger? I don't dwell on the whys and tell myself one day, someone will stay, or they won't.

While I'm completely distracted by my thoughts, the finish line sneaks up on me; Roxy is up ahead, crouched over, bouncing from one foot to the other in the ready position. I pick up speed and know it's time I have to push myself. I beg my mind to make my legs move as fast as they'll go. I use my arms to drive my legs forward. And then I pray that this last half mile, I don't trip and fall in front of thousands of people. Our hand-off is flawless, and she's gone, her long dark-brown ponytail swaying from left to right, and she quickly pulls away from the other ten lanes of runners.

I bend at the waist and rest my hands on my bent knees, trying to control my racing heart. I stand hunched over for a minute, inhaling deeply and allowing myself a slow exhale. I stay like this, frozen for a minute or two, and get lost, watching sweat fall from my face onto the dirt.

"Hey," a familiar voice pulls my attention from the dirt.

"Hey," I respond instinctively, then notice him standing above me. He's not dripping sweat or panting like I am. Nope, just standing there, smelling fresh and looking like the god he is.

"Xavier, what are you doing here?" I ask, trying to put a little distance between us, aware of I how I must smell.

"My work is sponsoring this event; I saw you run across the checkpoint from the tent over there." He nods toward his company's tent. "Do you want some water? We have an ice chest over there. Come on, you can sit down and rest while you wait for your partner."

I look up one last time to catch a glimpse of Roxy before she runs out of my sightline.

"Sure, why not," I reply, a smile creeping onto my face as I follow him, feeling a surge of unexpected excitement.

Chapter 4

Work is unusually hectic for a Sunday, and I find myself with zero patience for anyone today, which is not typical for me. I am sore from the race yesterday. I was supposed to be off work two hours ago, and to add to my frustration, I wasn't even supposed to work today. So, the fact that I'm here two hours later than scheduled adds to my frustration minute by minute. I allowed Philip to talk me into switching days off. He fed me some bullshit about a birthday party or baptism. Who knows? All their excuses run together these days.

Brightside, though, because I always look for the bright side of things, we sold thirty cars, and all the spiff money will buy me a few new pairs of shoes. Philip had coffee delivered this morning to say thank you for taking his shift, and he owes me lunch for a week. Favors don't come free around here.

Looking behind me but still progressing forward, I tell Bryan, "I'm going to walk the lot and make sure the guys are working."

Bryan jumps up and yells something incoherent at me just as I crash into something or someone.

"Ugh, I'm sorry," I say, embarrassed but more stunned.

A pair of giant hands grab me by my shoulders and push me just far enough backwards so I can see in his eyes. They're sky blue, like a clear day at the beach where no clouds exist.

"We need to stop meeting like this," Xavier says.

"Oh my God, Xavier, it's you; I'm so sorry. I'd love to say I'm much more graceful than this, but I haven't given you any reason to believe that," I say as my face flushes.

"Don't apologize. I think you got the worst end of me up and down."

In my head, I'm thinking, *Ummm, no, have you ever touched your chest? Can I snuggle up in the canyon between your pecs and live there?*

"Hi, I'm Bryan. I'm another sales manager here. It looks like you've met Joy, our resident clutz."

Xavier laughs and adds, "Yeah, we've met a few times, but lately, the meetings have been much more impactful," he says with a wink.

My face flushes again, and I know it shows. I have fair skin and freckles along my nose and cheeks. When I flush, there is zero chance of hiding it. Girls with champagne-colored hair and fair skin shouldn't flush.

"I'm assuming you're here to look at a car?" Bryan asks.

I manage to snap out of my trance when Bryan discreetly hits me in the arm.

"Ouch." I rub my arm. If I wasn't wholly humiliated before, I am now.

"I'm sorry," I say again. "I'm just distracted and hungry. Can I get a salesperson to help you?"

He quickly responds, "I hoped you could walk the lot with me. I think I'll be safer if I can keep an eye on you."

I look from him to Bryan as if I need Bryan's permission; he casually nods, giving me the go-ahead. I look at Xavier and say, "Sure, I'd be happy to show you around the lot."

Walking out of the lobby to the expansive car lot, I make a sweeping motion with my arm and ask Xavier, "So, what are you looking for?"

He looks down at me with a straight face and states the obvious, "A car."

So, I look up at him unamused and simply say, "You've come to the right place then." I can't tell if he's joking or serious.

He taps his chin thoughtfully with his index finger and adds, "I'm undecided about which one I want, but I think I'm leaning toward the Lexus ES."

"That's what I drive, and I love it. Would you like to take one on a test drive?"

Before he can answer, I ask, "Wait, doesn't Harper work at a dealership? Why aren't you buying a car from her?"

"Because she'll make me buy what she thinks is best for me and not what I want."

"Not shocked," I say under my breath.

He tilts his head and asks, "What's behind that comment?"

"Oh, nothing; she just comes off controlling like that."

His expression morphs from playful to defensive, and I suddenly feel very hot inside. Regretting the direction of this conversation, I ask, "What color car do you want to drive?"

"Does it matter?" he asks, and I'm unsure if his tone is one of confusion or irritation by my underhanded comment about Harper. So, I do what I do best: pretend everything is okay.

"Yes, it matters! Do you have to ask me that? Of course, it matters," I insist. Trying to make light of my shitty comment earlier, I add, "Harper hasn't taught you anything, has she?" I joke, and I give him a playful shove.

"It really does matter?" he asks, and some of the earlier tension has left his tone.

"No, of course, it doesn't matter. But when you buy a car, you want to buy the one you've test-driven," I say, laughing.

"Do you have one in black?" he asks with a playful return shove that tells me I didn't ruin this with my backhanded comment about Harper.

On the test drive, it takes everything out of me not to have him turn on a side street so I can have my way with him, but I make way too good money to give it all up for five minutes in the backseat of a Lexus. I catch him looking at me a few times out of the corner of his eye.

"You really should watch the road," I say with a flirty smile before I tell him everything he needs to know about the car.

He smiles at me and says, "You're better to look at."

And I can't help the flush that comes over my cheeks for the third time today.

His hand reaches out, lightly grazing my knee, catching me completely off guard. I'm momentarily stunned, my gaze fixed on him.

With a casual smile, he says, "I'm a touchy guy; I need to ensure I can reach my passenger comfortably while driving."

My mouth is suddenly the Sahara Desert, and I'm speechless. Unable to say anything, I nod.

"Are you okay?" he asks.

Stumbling over my words, I say, "Yes, you're perfect... Oh, I mean, I'm perfect." Cue blushing again.

I give him directions to a few more streets, trying to drag out this test drive as long as possible. But all too soon, before I want it to end, we find ourselves pulling back into the entry gate of the dealership.

The car buying process is usually long and drawn out, but this one feels over before it even starts. There is no negotiating. Bryan gives him everything at invoice because of our literal run-in. I'm sure I'll be the butt of jokes moving forward, but I'm used to it being the only girl with these guys, so I have thick skin.

When Xavier is done and ready to leave, I walk him out to his new car. He stops and leans casually on the driver's door, and his eyes meet mine with a steady, unwavering gaze filled with genuine warmth. There's a softness in his expression, making me feel truly seen. He's about to say something, but before he can speak, I take the opportunity to apologize for my underhanded comment earlier. "Xavier, I'm sorry for my comment about Harper earlier. I know you guys are tight, and that's not fair to you. She and I just never clicked."

He puts his finger under my chin, tilts my head to look at him, and says, "I know you and Harper have some bad blood between you. She stole your boyfriend—"

I interrupt him, "He wasn't my boyfriend."

"Right, he wasn't your boyfriend. At least, that's one thing you and Harper agree on." He nods then continues, "I don't care what Gabe was or wasn't to you. Harper is with him now, and that has to be hard for you; I get that. But Harper is my cousin and best friend, so underhanded comments don't sit well with me. Maybe you two can sit down and talk, and you'll realize that she's not as bad as you've made her out to be in your mind."

"No, I get it, and I'm sorry," I say, breaking eye contact.

"Look at me, Joy."

Instantly, I'm looking up at him, imprisoned by his blue eyes.

"It's okay, Joy," he says, reassuring me, and for some reason unbeknownst to me, I believe him.

Trying to diffuse some of the mounting sexual tension, I say, "I'm really sorry I ran into you again today. I am embarrassed. But hey, you know where to find me if you have questions about your car." I give him a playful wink. I'm stalling because the last thing I want is for this interaction right here to end.

"You said when I got here, you were supposed to be off two hours earlier, so if my math is correct, you haven't eaten in at least six hours." He crosses his arms in front of him and asks, "Can I buy you dinner?" His voice is smooth and confident.

My mind is screaming, *"Fuck Yes,"* but I'm trying not to portray the desperate girl that I am, so I play it cool and give him a composed nod. "Sure, that would be amazing. I'm starving."

Chapter 5

I follow him as we go to the outdoor mall near the dealership. I park next to him, and he quickly exits his vehicle to open my driver's door for me. When he takes my hand to help me out of my car, it's that same possessive, confident man who gave me advice a few days ago on the running trail, and I can't fight the internal swoon I'm feeling. As I look up to thank him, I notice he's wearing a playful grin, and that is the Xavier I know from when we would casually chat in passing when he'd visit Harper at my apartment building. Feeling insecure, I ask, "What's with the grin?"

He motions to our cars parked side by side, which are exactly the same. "His and hers," he says, matching his grinning expression.

I put my arm through his as we trek from the parking lot to the restaurant.

Once we are seated and have a minute to look over the menu, I fight the urge to order everything. I am starving but also trying to make a good impression, so I resist the temptation to indulge.

Xavier quickly looks over the menu and waves over to our server. "Can we order fries, mozzarella sticks, and fried pickles? And I'll have your house blonde on tap, and she'll have…" He motions in my direction, allowing me to order my drink.

Surprised by not only the number of appetizers he ordered but also the calorie count, I say, "Oh, um, I'll have the same thing he's having."

With our server off getting our order in, he says, "I didn't take you for a beer type of girl."

"Well, I didn't take you for a fried-food type of guy," I retort with the slightest tilt of my head.

Putting down his menu, he gives me his full attention. "I'm not usually; I just know you're hungry and figured you'd snack on one of those, so we don't have to rush this meal."

Who is this guy? Can we get married tonight and blow off all the dating bullshit? Fighting off the flush coming over me for the fifth time tonight, or perhaps the sixth time—I'm losing count—I smile and say, "Well, thank you. I love anything fried and anything sugar. That's why I run every day."

When our drinks and appetizers arrive, we fall back into conversation. It's enjoyable with Xavier. I don't feel nervous or uneasy; maybe that's because we've met a few times, or perhaps it's just him. Now I know why Harper has him around all the time.

Wiping the condensation on my beer glass with my fingertip, I say, "I know Harper is your cousin. Do you have siblings? Do you have any other cousins?"

"I had a brother; his name was Matthew. He died when he was eighteen."

I audibly gasp. "Oh my God, Xavier, I'm so sorry. I couldn't imagine that great of a loss." But I can. I lost my grandma when I was twenty years old.

Xavier looks down at the table and adds, "It was a long time ago."

"We don't have to talk about this," I interject quickly, trying not to dampen this evening.

"Joy, it's fine," he says, touching my hand from across the table. "I'm okay talking about it. Harper and I talk about him all the time. My brother may have died that day, but his memory is kept alive by talking about him."

"How did he die?" I quietly ask.

"Pneumonia," he says.

"Pneumonia," I repeat and raise my eyebrow in surprise. "I've never heard of someone so young dying of pneumonia."

"It's rare," he says. "He was otherwise healthy. He was at a friend's house and went home because he wasn't feeling well. He went straight to bed and never woke up again. Other than that, we don't have anymore more information. Harper and my brother were best friends growing up. I think part of her adolescence died that day."

"Closer than you and Harper?" I ask. From what I can see, Xavier and Harper are inseparable.

"We are closer now, but growing up, I was three years older than her, so her brother and I were close while she and Matthew were partners in crime. Our parents ensured they were in the same classes in school, they dressed alike, and did everything together since Harper didn't have many friends growing up."

I look at him, not expecting that. "What do you mean she didn't have friends?"

"Just that," he says as he leans back in his chair, taking a pull of his beer. "She didn't make friends easily growing up. She was comfortable with her family, which is all she felt she needed." He shrugs and continues, "There's more, but it's not my place to put her business on the street like that. I feel like I'm already toeing dangerous territory. If she finds out I was talking about her to you, she'd kick my ass." He laughs, but it doesn't seem to reach his eyes.

I motion my index finger across my sealed lips as if zipping them closed and say, "Your secret, *or hers*, is safe with me. And, if I'm being honest, I'm not surprised that Harper didn't have a lot of friends. She doesn't come off as the warmest human."

"Yeah." He rubs his chin. "She doesn't make it easy to get to know her, but once you do…" His voice trails off, his eyes flickering with a hint of resignation as if he knows that nothing he says will change my opinion of her.

Changing the subject, he asks, "Tell me about your family."

I laugh then ask, "Are you sure it's not too early in our friendship for that much drama?

He leans back and says, "Oh, now I'm intrigued. Do tell."

"Here goes," I say then take a deep breath, readying myself for a dive into the deep end. "I have five siblings that I've met less than a handful of times."

'What?" His brow furrows, and his eyes narrow. "How does that even happen?"

"I've always referred to myself as my dad's dirty little secret."

He tilts his head, studying me.

I continue, "He lives in Iowa and is a doctor. He has five amazing children that he and his wife dote over. I've visited them maybe four times in my entire life. My grandparents were teachers, so in the summer, they'd pack me up in their RV, and we'd drive across the country so I could see them. God forbid my dad splurge for the two-hundred dollar plane ticket so he could see his "other" daughter. I would've never seen him growing up if it weren't for my grandparents. Have you heard enough, or do you want me to go on?" I ask, trying to read his expression.

"I'm invested now, girl. Don't stop. Tell me everything," he says as he leans forward onto the table. He looks me dead in the eyes, and their clear blue color takes my breath away.

With another deep inhale, I continue, "When I was eighteen, I flew out to see them on my dime. My sister had a pretty serious illness, and I wanted to be there for her; I wanted to be there with all of them. Looking back, it was stupid. I don't have a relationship with her, my dad, or his wife. They didn't want me there and made zero effort to make me feel like part of the family. We went to dinner after leaving the hospital the night I got there, and we ran into some of my dad's friends. When he was forced to introduce me because the awkwardness was too apparent to ignore, he stammered over his words, and I honestly think he forgot my name for a minute.

"The introduction went something like, 'Um, oh yeah, um, this is my um daughter from California.'

"I saved the blundering idiot and said, 'Nice to meet you; my name is Joy.'

"The kicker was when his friend said, 'I had no idea you had a daughter in California.'

"He didn't mean he didn't know one of my dad's kids lived in California. He thought my dad only had five kids; he'd clearly never mentioned his sixth child. Hearing the astonishment in his friend's voice and the shame on my dad's face was a punch to the gut like I'd never experienced. It's one thing to know someone doesn't want you or is embarrassed by you, but seeing it play out in real-time is just too much."

Heat rises to the surface of my cheeks. "I haven't been back to Iowa to see my dad or siblings since that interaction, and I have zero desire ever to return."

Xavier is just sitting here listening intently, his eyes barely blinking, wide in astonishment. He refuses to look away from me. He's sat here hanging on every one of my words. For the first time in my life, I feel heard. He's made me feel heard, and that's a very scary feeling to accept.

Chapter 6

I've never had sex on the first date. I'm twenty-four years old, and I'm still a first-date virgin, but with how this man looks at me when I talk to him, that could very well change tonight. Xavier is gorgeous, too gorgeous for me. Self-esteem usually isn't an issue for me. I'm comfortable with my appearance, but when he rises from the table and pulls my chair out, I feel tiny. He stands six feet tall, towering at least seven inches above me. As I glance up at him, I take a step back, feeling his presence envelop me.

When he takes my hand in his, it's completely engulfed, and I can't help but notice the definition in his massive arms. I swallow hard, my mind wandering to thoughts I need to shake away. As he leads me from the table, I get a waft of his cologne – it's clean, not overwhelming. Hints of sandalwood and pine blend perfectly, making him smell as masculine as he looks.

After he pays the bill and walks me to my car, I have an eternal battle rising up inside my body. There are butterflies taking flight in my stomach and panic raging war in my head. And let's not mention the pounding in my lady parts that have been dormant since Gabe and I ended things.

Half of me – the irrational side – wants to take him home and fuck him until I forget what day it is. The other half – hello, Ms. Rational – says that's a very horrible idea.

As we step outside the restaurant, the cool evening air wraps around us, a stark contrast to the warmth from inside. We slowly walk to my car, the silence between us charged with unspoken anticipation.

In the parking lot, I suggest, "Should we exchange numbers?"

He waves me off with a confident smile. "I already have yours from your business card, and I know where you work."

"Right," I softly say, turning to face him. The parking lot lights cast a soft glow, highlighting the angles of his face and the intensity in his eyes.

I reach for my car door, my hand trembling slightly. As I fumble with the handle, he steps closer, his presence overpowering me once again. I look up, caught in his gaze, and I feel the magnetic pull between us.

"Thank you for dinner," I manage to whisper, my voice betraying me.

"You're welcome," he replies, his voice low and steady. There's a moment of hesitation, a fleeting pause that feels like the world has stopped spinning for just a second.

Instead of replying further, he takes another step closer, closing the barely there distance between us. His hand reaches out, brushing a strand of hair from my face. The touch is electric, and then, without another word, he leans in. His lips meet mine in a soft, tender kiss that takes my breath away. Everything around us fades, leaving only the sensation of his kiss and the warmth of his touch on me. I wrap my arms around his neck, requiring me to stand on my toes. I beg my legs not to fail me.

The remnants of his beer invade my senses when he allows my tongue entrance into his mouth. I get lost in his kiss, pushing all thoughts from my mind. I don't want any distractions to ruin this kiss. He pushes against my pelvis, and oh god, he's definitely aroused too.

He pulls his head away, taking those delicious lips with him. Damn it. Then he straightens his arms and holds me at arm's length. "I'm going to let you get into your car before we do something you're not ready to do."

My whole body screams, *Hello, my body and I are ready. My God, we are ready*! Begrudgingly, I say, "Um, yeah, you're right." It comes out more breathless than I would've liked. I lower myself into my car and watch as he stands there until I pull away.

The following day at work, two dozen pink and red roses are mixed in a large clear glass vase sitting at my desk with a card that reads, *Thank you for letting me get to know you.*

I sink into my chair with a heavy sigh. It's a gesture, no doubt, but one that leaves me feeling apprehensive. Last night with Xavier was wonderful – he is great, and when he kissed me, I felt a rush of emotion I've never experienced before. Yet, as I drove home, a sense of unease settled over my life, a dark cloud. Xavier seems too good to be true, and deep down, I can't shake the fear that he's a heartbreak waiting to happen. Life has taught me one thing for certain: if someone is going to get hurt, it'll be me.

This public display of affection draws the attention of the girls in the business office and all the sales guys.

"So, if I want flowers, all I have to do is run into guys in the middle of the dealership," a receptionist jokes.

"Ha-ha," I say, unamused. It's too early for all these questions and this much attention.

"Ugh," I mutter under my breath. "It's going to be a long day."

"Joy, you're the only girl on earth who isn't happy about

getting flowers at work," Roxanne says from behind me.

I jump and clench my chest. "Who let you out of your dungeon?"

She rarely comes out of the business office, let alone spends time in the mangers' office.

"I saw flowers getting delivered and had to see who they were for," she says before she takes an exaggerated sniff of a rosebud. "Imagine my surprise when they were addressed to my best friend! And here I was thinking I knew every about you." She narrows her eyes playfully, a smirk forming on her lips. "You conveniently forgot to mention a guy sending you flowers? And after all my lectures about you dating! Are you holding out on me?"

"No, I'm not holding out on you, and it's not that I'm not happy to get flowers, but the gesture is way over the top."

"Well, who are they from?" Roxanne asks, hands on her hips.

"Lower your voice! You're making a scene."

"Girl, do you want me to make a scene?"

"This is why they keep you locked up all day in the back! Do you remember me telling you about Xavier, Harper's cousin?"

"Are you having sex with her cousin to piss her off for stealing Gabe? Joy, you are not this diabolical."

"No!" I say as I drag her by the arm from the manager's office into the restroom. Even though they're public, it's safer here than in front of everyone. "A few days ago, when you and I met up for a run, I ran into him on the way back—like literally ran into him. Then he appeared at the end of the relay race out of thin air smelling like a dream. He offered me shade and water. And yesterday, he showed up to buy a car." He's everywhere I am.

"Why didn't he buy a car from Harper?" she interrupts.

"I asked the same thing!" I say, almost jumping up and

down, feeling validated by Roxy's questions. "Anyway, that's not important. After he bought the car, he asked me to dinner, and we made out in the parking lot," I say in a mumble.

"You made out with him?" she shouts.

"Roxanne, I'm going to murder you if you keep yelling," I say, covering her mouth.

"Okay, so why are we not happy?" she mumbles through my hand still covering her mouth.

I remove my hand, and she tilts her head, eyebrows raised dangerously high.

"Again, it's not that I'm not happy, but the last time a guy sent me flowers at work, he broke up with me for another girl. It was a simple dinner date, and I'm trying to control my emotions. That's all. Besides, Xavier is a nice guy, but he's way too hot for me, and his cousin is Harper."

She grins before adding, "If what you say about Harper is true, could you imagine the look on her face if she sees you with her cousin?"

I shove her and laugh. "You know I hate you, right?"

"That's okay. I have enough love for both of us. But seriously, stop running away from happiness. If a guy sends you flowers, stop stressing and smell the roses."

At lunch, my phone vibrates with an unknown number. With practiced ease, I answer the phone in my best professional voice. "Hello, this is Joy." And make a mental note to push for a work phone so I don't keep getting calls from customers.

"Hey, Joy, it's Xavier. Are you hungry?"

"Oh, hi, Xavier. I just realized I never got your number last night."

"I didn't give it to you because I had every intention of calling today."

And here is the first face flush of the day. I hope this doesn't become a daily thing.

I gulp before quietly asking, "What do you have in mind?" This guy took me to dinner last night, then surprised me (and anyone who walks by my desk) with flowers and now lunch. This doesn't feel like Mr. Right Now, but Mr. Right and that's terrifying; I'm not ready for Mr. Right. I should say no? Yes, I'll say I'm too busy and suggest a raincheck.

"I was thinking something fried." He laughs, snapping me out of my thoughts. "I work close to you; I can be there in ten minutes," he says.

"Sure, I'll meet you out front," I say before I can stop myself. I end the call and groan into my hands.

He pulls up in his new black Lexus, and I jump into the passenger seat. His car smells like him already—I don't think he's even had it for twenty-four hours. The scent is so enchanting that it makes me forget how to speak. He looks so good in his long black button-down suit shirt, sleeves rolled up to his elbows, black suit pants, and designer shoes. When I look up at his face, all I see are his bright blue eyes.

He turns to me and asks, "Do you feel like anything specific?"

"What?" I ask.

"Lunch. Does anything sound good?" he says with a raised eyebrow.

The one thing I hate more than confrontation is deciding what to eat or where to eat. It's stressful, and I'd rather starve than make those decisions for a group.

"Oh, no… I'm good with whatever you want." I look down to my hands in my lap.

"You sure?" he says with a smile.

"Positive. Whatever you want is good with me," I reply.

A few minutes later, we pull up to a very familiar pizza restaurant. Sports teams take over the restaurant every Saturday and Sunday. After soccer games growing up, my team would always come here. All the parents would order pizza and beer, and the kids would play games and run wild. I'd go when my grandma could drive me, but it wasn't often.

This is the last place I expected Xavier to choose, but I'm also assuming this won't be the last time this man surprises me.

"Is this okay?" he asks as we head for the entrance.

"It's perfect. I love it," I say. "I love hot pizza, greasy pizza, cold pizza, day-old pizza... *any* type of pizza."

We maneuver our way through the zig-zag line until we reach the register to order. Glancing at the menu that spans the entire front of the house, I order a small cheese pizza with red peppers, bell peppers, and olives.

He looks at me, and I shrug and say, "I know, oddly specific."

He orders a pepperoni pizza. We find a private booth in the restaurant's corner near a large window overlooking the parking lot.

"Nice view huh?" I say trying to lighten the mood as we settle into our seats.

"Yeah, it's pretty nice. I always like places with big windows," he replies, glancing outside.

"How's the first day in your car?" I ask, smiling a bit.

"I'm happy with it so far, I had a good salesperson," he says with a wink.

Before I can question his basic topping choice for his pizza, he blurts out, "Last night, when we were leaving the restaurant, was it too much too fast?" He scratches the back of his neck.

Confused, I ask, "What do you mean?"

"We don't know each other that well." His voice is tinged with nervousness, a stark contrast to his usually confident demeanor. "We went out once and had a great time. I want to make sure it wasn't too much for you too soon," he says, his voice quieter now. His eyes dart away, unable to hold my gaze, and his shoulders slump slightly. The confident, possessive guy I know seems to have vanished, replaced by someone unsure and vulnerable.

A little blunter than I expected. I ask, "Are you saying that for my benefit, or is that how you feel?"

He stammers, "I... I don't want you to feel like I'm coming on too strong or things are moving too quickly." He plays with our table number.

"Xavier, if you asked me to go home with you last night, I can't say I would've turned you down. Please don't be worried about me."

He opens his mouth but no words come out, and for the first time in my life, I feel like I'm in control of something bigger than me. I've never been the one in power.

Throwing caution to the wind, I add, "So, you don't have to worry about my feelings. I'm pretty open with what I want regarding men and relationships."

Again, he doesn't say anything for a good few moments before he asks, "What are you doing Friday night?"

I think he's being facetious, but I don't know him well enough to read more into the comment. His face isn't giving anything away.

"I promised my best friend a girl's night, but depending on how drunk we get, maybe we'll meet after?"

Come hell or high water, I will see Xavier Friday night.

Chapter 7

Roxanne and I FaceTime the entire ride to our favorite bar that is ideally located between our two apartments. We picked this as our bar, so neither of us has a longer Uber ride than the other. Just like so many times before we arrive at our bar simultaneously and hug like we didn't just see each other at work three hours ago.

Even though Roxy and I work together, we're in different departments. She spends her days in the business office, tucked away in the back of the dealership, handling paperwork and finances. I, on the other hand, avoid that area like plague, preferring to stay out front with the sales teams. She's my savior at work, though. She does anything I need, which makes my life a million times easier.

Roxanne is wearing a short-fitted red dress with nude heels. I have a short, tight, black, long-sleeved dress that has a low V showing all my cleavage. Seeing her in red makes me wish I was more comfortable wearing color in my wardrobe. I always buy a new color shirt or skirt, which sits in the back of my closet and collects dust. During my entire adolescent years, I wore black and rocked a grunge style. Some habits take time to break.

Opting not to sit at the bar tonight, we grab a table, order drinks and catch up on life outside work. "What's up with Christopher?" I ask.

"He came back, begging for forgiveness." She shows me a large rock in her left hand.

"Shut the F up!" I yell. "When did this happen, and why am I just hearing about it? I saw you three ago at work."

"Do you think I would tell you something this important at work? He returned two days ago and said he needed to show me how serious he was about us, so this was his grand gesture. I kept it to myself until I could tell you in person. You're the first person I've told, and it's been killing me. I almost slipped a thousand times the first day alone. But seeing your face right now makes it worth the wait," she says with a smile.

I'm speechless. I'm staring at her hand with my mouth agape. I finally manage to say, "I'm shaking right now. I can't believe he grew a pair and finally asked you to marry him. I'm so excited for you! How are we going to tell your parents? Did you set a date? How did he propose? Girl, start talking!" I say as I'm holding her arms from across the table, franticly shaking them in excitement.

"Okay, okay, slow down… I told you he was texting me the day of the race."

"No, you didn't, but we'll address that later."

She rolls her eyes and continues, "He knew he made a mistake right away. He didn't want to break up and bombarded me with texts all day, which I ignored."

I raise my glass in solidarity, and we clink glasses.

She resumes, "When I got home, he was at my door with flowers and invited me to an early dinner. I was too tired to go out, so we ordered pizza; he met the delivery guy at the door, put my ring on that white thing that keeps the box from hitting the cheese, and when I opened the box, there it was, and he was down on one knee." She shrugs nonchalantly.

I look off into the distance and say, "Pizza and diamonds. I knew Chris was the perfect guy."

We laugh; she almost pushes me off my barstool and then continues answering the rest of my questions. "We're not waiting; there's no reason to. We've been together forever… And I don't want to wait."

There's more to it, but I don't want to wait for a statement that she'll never admit. She's afraid his ex will come around again, and he'll choose her. Are her insecurities a good enough reason to get married? Probably not, but I keep those opinions to myself.

There's a dull ache in my chest right now. I'm so happy for Roxy. This is everything she's always wanted. She's the girl you marry and build a life with. She will be the perfect wife and mother. But my reality looks different than hers. The thought of being single forever sits heavy on my heart. Roxanne and Christopher won't wait to have kids, either. I assume she'll make Chris put a baby in her on their honeymoon. I'm a girl's girl. I don't usually feel sorry for myself, especially when my friends have such great news, but it's at this moment I feel like everyone is moving forward, and no matter how fast I run, I can't keep up. I snap out of my private pity party before she notices and quickly ask, "Can we wear black bridesmaid dresses?"

She raises her brows and smiles.

I put my hands together and beg. "Please don't make me wear some pink tool monstrosity."

"Joy," Roxy says as she reaches across the table and grabs my hand.

I have to bite the side of my cheek to distract myself from

the overwhelming urge I have to cry. She can see all my fears written across my face without me having to say a word, I know it.

She says, "First, I'm not getting pregnant right away; second, you'll never be alone; third, you can wear whatever you want when you stand beside me before my family and our friends. And lastly, speaking of monstrosity, how is our flower guy?"

"He's fine," I say, trying to skip past her question and not talk about me. Quickly, I add, "I don't want you to think I'm anything but ecstatic for you. More often than not, I feel stagnated, and then major life events reiterate my fears of being alone."

Roxy says, "No way, Joy! We have two things happening right now. Both are equally important but completely separate conversations. So, I'll give you the authority to pick the one we discuss first."

"I prefer not to talk about either, but we can talk about the flowers because I don't want to talk about my insecurities, not tonight, okay."

"Okay," she says in her very soft, sincere voice. Roxy has always been soft-spoken, which is crazy since she was raised in a house with a handful of Hellion siblings.

She picks up, not missing a beat. "Tell me about this run-in with Xavier last week?" she insists.

I groan and shake my head. "I was digging through my backpack to check your text and make sure you were okay, then—bam! I collided with his sweaty chest. It was amazing." I chuckle.

But Roxanne is staring at me. Her eyes are half-closed, her forehead creased in confusion, and she's nodding along as if trying to wrap her brain around the story.

Trying not to leave anything out, I quickly add the remainder of our interactions under my breath, "Then lunch the next day."

"What!" she yells, and a few heads turn toward us. She can't care less. "*And*," she draws out for effect.

"And he's freaking gorgeous. He's a heartbreak waiting to happen. I can feel it in my bones. He's too good for me," I say, sliding down my chair and attempting to shrink into the table.

"Shut up, Joy, I'm serious."

Heads turn in our direction yet again. *Where has my soft-spoken Roxy gone. please?*

I continue, "No, no, wait, hear me out. He's perfect. He has a big personality, you know, super outgoing, charming as hell, so sweet, and not a hint of an ego. I feel like I'll get lost in his big personality, like I won't be able to keep up with him, or I won't be enough."

"So, you're going to self-sabotage so you can't get hurt. Will you shut down like you do with every other guy?" she says with way too much attitude.

"No, I'm actually going to fuck him every opportunity I get, and I'll try my best to keep him at arm's length, so I don't get hurt," I say with a smug tone, then lift my hand to the air for her a high five, which she doesn't reciprocate so I high five myself.

"You know I'll always be here to catch you if you fall," she says sweetly.

"I know, friend, and that's why no one will ever replace you."

Chapter 8

few hours and too many drinks later, I'm in my Uber and decide to text Xavier.

Me – What are you doing?

Xavier – Truth - Or play it cool?

Me – Truth always.

Xavier – Pacing my apartment, hoping you'd text me. *He adds the emoji with the hand hitting his forehead.*

Me – You know where I live. Do you want to meet me there?

He's waiting at my door when I get off the elevator. He's wearing black jeans and a short-sleeved, navy-blue button-down shirt. His biceps are so big they're straining his shirt hem.

He looks me up and down a few times and smiles. "You look amazing, Joy," he says.

"So do you," I reply, sure liquid courage is the only thing keeping me this confident.

We just stand there looking at each other as the tension grows so thick between us that it's hard to breathe. "So…" he says, very devilish, moving closer to me slowly.

"So…" I draw out, feeling him move in closer and closer as he gently pushes me against my door. His presence looms over me, overwhelming and somewhat intimidating. I start to regret the confidence I had yesterday with him. I am so fucking nervous that I literally can't feel my fingertips. Maybe that's the drinks Roxanne and I had earlier I don't know. There are so many emotions right now.

I fumble for my keys, fingers trembling as I locate them in my bag, then I reach behind me to unlock the door. He doesn't move an inch, forcing us to share the same space and breathe the same air. I finally fit my key into the lock; his front is pressed against me, still pinning my back to the door. I turn the knob, and the door opens. He leads me in, his closeness compelling me to walk backward, his body still refusing to allow any space to come between us. Once we're inside, he kicks the door closed behind us.

He gently pushes my hair off my shoulder, and kisses it. Fire erupts in my stomach. He trails his way up and kisses my neck. Every hair on my body stands at attention. He continues to kiss me; I tilt my head to the side, allowing him better access to it. He then shifts to my cheek, softly kissing it. I can hardly breathe. My heart is pounding so hard that there's no way he can't feel it against him. He leisurely relocates from my cheek and kisses the side of my mouth as if asking for permission to proceed to what we both know is next. He gives me a peck on my lips, and I instantly feel it between my legs. I can't take it anymore. I have to kiss him back. I kiss his bottom lip, taking it in my mouth and tugging on it. Then I take his top lip. He bites my lower lip into his mouth. I sense a tremor in my knees, a subtle betraying quiver. There's no way I'm not letting Xavier fuck me tonight. I deliberately pull away and lead him through the living room, past my dining area, and down the hallway that leads directly to my bedroom. He gently pulls my dress over my head, and the anticipation only makes me think I'm going to have a fucking heart attack.

He unclasps my bra and gingerly shimmies my panties down my legs, never taking his eyes off mine. I follow his lead, unbuttoning his shirt and pulling it off him. Damn, he is so hot. I unbuckle his belt and then unfasten his pants. I'm still not taking my eyes off his. He unzips his pants, and I break his stare. I can see the outline of his cock in his black boxers, and wetness starts to drip down my thighs. I could orgasm just looking at him. God, I hope I don't embarrass myself.

He slides his index finger down my slit, and the contact makes me jump a little. He rubs it back and forth, with the perfect amount of pressure that forces me to move my hips in sync with his rhythm.

He moans, "Joy, you're so wet; you feel so good."

I lower his boxers to the floor, and my knees follow them to the floor. His cock is big in size and girth, but I take it all in my mouth. I don't go slow; I take it all in, and he moans, "Oh fuck, that feels amazing."

He takes my hair and holds onto it as I slide his cock from the front of my mouth to the back of my throat. I pull it out and take the crown of it in and out, faster and faster. I flick it with my tongue, and he squirms inside my mouth. He's trying to push it further into my mouth to release the pressure from the tip, but I don't let him. I keep flicking back and forth. My thighs are getting wetter and wetter. I try to rub them together for a bit of friction, just to satisfy some of the pulsating in my clit. After a few more seconds, I retake his entire length, and another moan escapes him.

"Joy, I can't take any more. Please let me have you. Are you on birth control?"

"Yes," I say, breathless.

"I'm going to take you bare. Are you okay with that?" His voice is strangled and needy.

"Yes." That is all I can manage to say again.

He grabs a handful of my hair and pulls me to his lips. He shoves his tongue in my mouth as if he owns me, then he picks me up just below my ass, and I wrap my legs around his waist. He carries me to a wall adjacent to my bed, pushes my back against it, and enters me with such vigor I lose my breath.

"Do you like that, baby?" he whispers.

"Yes, God, Yes," I say, breathless as my blood pulses through my body, refusing to slow down.

He thrusts a little slower, pulling his entire length from me and then back in. He uses the wall and his body to hold me up and his finger to rub my swollen clit.

It takes only a few strokes, and I'm on the brink of an orgasm. "Don't stop," I say. "Oh God, please don't stop," I'm begging now.

He continues his assault on my pussy, and I'm shuttering inside as my orgasm fully erupts, and pleasure fills my body. I scream, and my body squeezes around him. "Xavier, yes, oh god, yes."

His moans intensify with my orgasm as my pussy clenches around him and my nails bite into his skin. With a few more punishing thrusts, he bites my shoulder and he releases himself in me. He holds me close to him, sweat the only thing between us. His voice is strangled when he whispers, "You're amazing, baby; I want to do this with you forever."

With that one sentence, my entire mindset about life shifts. I'm not sure I can breathe without this man. And that realization scares the hell out of me. I have no idea how he even really feels about me. We just started talking a few days ago. How did I go from running into him on the trail to *I think I'm falling in love*? The thought terrifies me.

Chapter 9

As I ride down the elevator to meet Roxanne for our day of dress shopping, my phone vibrates with a text. Xavier - *I can't wait to celebrate your birthday tonight after your wedding dress shopping spree.*

I lock my phone and shove it into my purse, take a deep breath, and lean against the rail, resting my head against the mirrored walls. It's been a whirlwind two weeks. In the short time Xavier and I have been talking, he's been everything a girl could ever dream of, so how do I tell him I don't celebrate my birthday?

I jump into Roxy's car, and she's already signing Happy Birthday to me and shoving a cupcake in my face before I can shut the door.

"Give me a second to get settled before you vomit birthday cheer all over me."

"Um, this is *our* day, Joy. You're not allowed to be bossy or grouchy, so let's hash this out now."

"You're right. I'm sorry," I say in my overly excited voice.

"Start talking," Roxanne demands.

"Xavier still wants to take us out for my birthday tonight."

"Yes, and? We're still going right because I brought my

dinner dress. You are not taking this away from me, are you? I need a fancy dinner and a night out," she begs.

"How do I tell him why I don't celebrate my birthday?"

"You can start with the truth, but can it wait until after dinner? I'll never have an opportunity to eat there again."

"What, just tell him my grandma died the day after my twentieth birthday, and it's a horrible reminder that I have no family and only one friend in my life?"

"It's a start," she says, not taking her eyes off the road.

My grandparents were my life growing up. Telling everyone I loved her feels such an understatement. My grandfather was retired by the time I came along. He was in some branch of the military that earned him a Purple Heart. He was a good man but not as involved with raising me as my grandma was. I think he was so tired from raising my mom and didn't have the energy to deal with me.

My grandma was a Girl Scout leader, which made me one by default. Girl Scouts was NOT my thing, but being with my grandma was. My grandfather died when I was sixteen, so he got to miss me jumping his bronco on rollerblades, getting in a fight with a girl from the bus, putting my fist through her window, and, of course, playing soccer every weekend. Yeah, I was a lot.

I got pregnant when I was seventeen years old. I chose not to confide in anyone and dealt with it on my own. The process was oddly simple, almost a little too easy. Looking back, I suspect my grandma would've been disappointed in me, but that's another conversation I'll never have with her. As an adult, my views have shifted about pregnancy. I've learned to take responsibility for myself now. I waiver back and forth about my decision as a seventeen-year-old girl. Was getting an abortion avoiding responsibility or a necessary decision given my circumstances? Sadly, I couldn't raise a kid; my mom couldn't help me. My grandma was devastated by the death of my grandpa. It's a chapter in my life I rarely revisit and a chapter I never talk about.

"Earth to Joy," Roxy says as she waves her hand in front of my face.

"Oh, sorry."

"Just reliving the shittiest day of your life?" she asks.

"And some," I reply. "The saying is true about never really knowing what the day will bring because on that day, the last thing I expected was my grandma dying."

"Yeah," she says in a somber tone. "I'll never forget that phone call." She places a comforting hand on my leg, but quickly withdraws it to steer us into a large parking lot that is flanked by several different stores.

Roxanne drives in circles for a few minutes, looking for parking, and my mind wanders again.

My mom called me with the news, which just fed my resentment toward her. I hated my mom; she was the last person I wanted to talk to during a tragedy. I hung up and looked at Roxanne from across my desk. Her eyes were wild with concern, pleading for an explanation of what had just transpired between my mom and me.

My grandma never woke up after surgery. I sat next to her body, which was only working because of the beeping machines that could drive any sane person crazy after a day. Pumps filled her lungs; tubes fed her oxygen and fluids. *Beep, beep, beep.* I watched her blood pressure and oxygen for hours—*beep, beep, beep.* With every beep, I would plead with her to wake up.

"Grandma, can you hear me?" I kept saying on repeat in a panic.

"Grandma, if you don't wake up, they're going to pull you

off life support, and I can't be left here without you."

I have never cried so hard, and I don't think I'll ever cry like that again. My eyes are almost swollen shut, heavy, as if my lids were having a battle of wills with gravity.

"If you can hear me, please squeeze my hand," I begged her. I used everything in my being to will her to squeeze my hand and give me a fucking sign that she wasn't going to die and leave me alone in this world.

We buried her a week later. I knew I'd never be the same.

The second reason I don't celebrate my birthday is that the two people who brought me into this world never wanted me.

"So, are we going to be honest with him or lie?" Roxanne pulls me from my thoughts for the second time today.

Startled, I look over to her. "I don't know," I say as we get out of the car and walk across the large parking lot to a pristine white building with a massive double-door entry and a gold sign that reads "*The Blushing Bride.*" The closer we get to the building, the mannequins come into focus, all adorned in elaborately beaded dresses in different shades of white and creams.

"Joy, what is the real reason you don't want to go to dinner for your birthday? I know you don't like to celebrate your birthday, but *we* do. Why are you avoiding this?"

"What if it's too much for him? What if I'm too much for him? What if I leave like everyone else leaves me? I was born to two people who didn't want me. My birthday is an annual reminder of how I'm not good enough and I'll never be good enough for the two people who are supposed to love me unconditionally. Why would a guy like Xavier stay?"

She stops, her hand resting on the large, gold door handle of the building. "And that's the truth right there. How long have we been friends?"

"I don't know? Forever. Why?" I ask looking down at my shoes.

"Have I ever left you?"

"No," I answer in an even more reserved voice now.

"Joy, your parents are assholes. You were dealt a shitty hand, but let's face it, grandparents die; it's part of life. Shit, best friends die, but if you keep allowing your past rejections and tragedies to dictate and control your future, then you might as well be buried next to your grandma because this is right here"—she motions her hand around me—"is not living."

I look at her, place my hand over her hand still on the door, and pull it open. As the doors open, the air conditioner rushes out as if it's been trapped in there trying to get out. The cool air calms my nerves.

I look to Roxanne and say, "Today is your day. Can we not talk about my shitty childhood and drink some free champagne and try on some sexy wedding dresses, please?"

"I thought you'd never ask."

Chapter 10

After a long day of shopping and champagne, Roxanne and I decide to meet Xavier and Christopher at the steakhouse since the dress shop is halfway to LA, where Johnston Steakhouse is located. Johnston's is a three-Michelin-star restaurant. The waitlist for a reservation is months long, so I have no idea how Xavier managed to get us a table on such short notice. Pulling up to the valet in Roxanne's Honda Civic is the most ironic scene I've seen play out before me, but on par for the two of us, we couldn't care less what other people think of us. Stepping out of her car, we're both wearing sleek black dresses, hers long-sleeved, mine short and strapless.

Roxanne is positively beaming with excitement. Her love for food and restaurants is unmatched. If she could afford it, she'd dine somewhere new every night. Add 'fancy' in front of the restaurant, and you've made her year. Roxanne hurries around the car and puts her arm through mine. "This is so awesome; I can't wait to get inside."

"Yay, me too," I say in a mocking tone.

"She holds my arm tighter and whispers, "Xavier worked hard to make this happen; we agreed you wouldn't ruin it for us. Promise you won't say anything to him at dinner; tell him at home tonight if you decide to be truthful."

"I know, Mother," I reply with a guilty smile. "I'll be on my best behavior," I say, my tone tinged with amusement.

Our laughter fills the air as we walk along the red velvet runner that leads us to the grand entrance of the restaurant.

Just shy of our reservation, we meet up with the guys. As I approach Xavier, his eyes sweep over me, and the grin he offers makes celebrating my birthday worth every emotional headache. Roxanne hits my arm repeatedly, gesturing toward Christopher. He's talking to Xavier, who's dressed in a black suit paired with a navy shirt and tie. The combination brings out the depth of his blue eyes. His hair is meticulously styled, boasting a thick side parting reminiscent of a 1950s' gangster. Towering tall at six foot five inches, it's impossible to miss him in a crowd. I lean into Roxanne and whisper, "He cleans up real nice, doesn't he?"

Once I make my way through the crowd and to him, he wraps me in a tight embrace and whispers, "I get to take that dress off you tonight, right?"

Roxanne clears her throat to get our attention. We both look at her, and she says, "Our table is ready." She motions her head in the direction of our table.

I'm keenly aware that I still haven't told Xavier the truth about why I don't celebrate my birthday. (or even that I don't at all.)

Once seated, Chris leans across our small table. "Xavier, how did you manage to get us in tonight?"

"I have a friend through work who owed me a favor. Joy's birthday was a perfect time to cash in on it." He inclines into me, wraps his arm around my shoulder, and gives me a wink.

Nodding in agreement, Christopher asks, "So Joy was okay

with allowing you to take her out to dinner on her birthday?"

Xavier's eyebrows knit together, his forehead furrowing deeply. His eyes dart between the three of us, searching for answers. "What do you mean?" he asks, looking between the three of us.

And, being completely clueless, Chris says, "Well, Joy doesn't celebrate her birthday."

"You don't?" he asks, his eyebrows almost touching his hairline. "Why did I not know this?"

Roxy interjects and says, "Joy doesn't like people to make a big deal about her birthday, so we usually do something small."

"That's not why," Chris argues.

I kick him under the table.

"Ouch!" he says as he rubs his shin.

"For Christ's sake, Christopher." Roxy scolds, "Just shut the fuck up about her birthday."

"What did I miss?" Xavier asks as he looks at me for answers. "Why didn't you tell me you don't celebrate your birthday?"

The look on his face hits me at full force. I feel shitty that I hurt his feelings for not being honest with him.

Trying to defuse the situation like I always do, I casually say, "Xavier, I usually don't make a big deal about my birthday. It's not a big deal. Can we order already? I'm starving."

Roxy gives me the stink eye from across the table, cluing me in that the last statement that came out sounded different in reality than it did in my head.

Xavier raises his eyebrows again for the second time tonight and gives me a curt, "Okay, that explains nothing." Then he directs his attention to Christopher and asks, "Are you excited about the wedding?"

Chris puts his arm around Roxanne and pulls her in close. "Who wouldn't be anxious to make this girl their old lady."

"Classy," she says as she shoves him off her. "I hope that's not part of your vows."

"Wait, let me get a picture of you two," I say, stretching behind my chair for my purse. I grab my phone and lean my back into the aisle, aiming for the perfect shot. I momentarily forget that it's not just an aisle but also a pathway for foot traffic. I accidentally collide with a passing waiter, causing a waterfall of seven very cold ice waters to come crashing down over my head.

A young, very panicked waiter yells, "Ma'am, I'm so sorry," as he attempts to towel dry my once perfectly curled hair with a napkin from our table. His ceaseless apologies draw the attention of the entire restaurant, and what was embarrassment seconds ago has morphed into mortification.

I look across the table to Roxanne for help, but nope. She's laughing hysterically, tears running down her face. Trying to keep my composure, I slowly slide my chair out, grab my purse, excuse myself from the table, and make my way to the restroom. After a few seconds, Roxanne comes barreling through the doors.

"Oh my God, are you okay?" She's still laughing.

"Stop laughing, or I will leave this restaurant right now."

"You can't. I drove, and all your shit is in my car." And she's still laughing.

"This is a fucking disaster," I hiss.

"Is it a disaster?" she asks, still laughing.

"What do you mean, is it a disaster? Yes, it's a fucking disaster. Look at me!" I shout as I move my arms up and down my soaked body.

"We must have different ideas of what a disaster is." She's still laughing. "Okay," she says as she pushes her dress down and glides her hands through her hair. I think I'm done laughing, not at you, but with you."

"I'm not laughing, Roxanne."

"But you should be, Joy. It's your birthday. I want you to fall in love with the thought of your birthday again," she says without a care in the world like I didn't just get not one, but *seven* glasses of water dumped on my head.

I shake my head as she reaches into her purse and grabs a scrunchie and a brush.

She hands them to me and says, "Slick your hair back into a pony, add some red lipstick, and put more mascara on. This will all look intentional in two minutes."

"Do I have to go back out there?" I whine as I look into the mirror, fixing my slick-back ponytail.

"Yes, you look perfect. Now, let's go eat our food," she says, dismissing my pout.

Making our way back through the restaurant between the tables that are placed too close for comfort, as proven by the waterfall that just came crashing over my head, I lean close to Roxanne and whisper, "Everyone is staring at us."

"No, Joy, they're staring at you," she says, laughing again. "Just think your ice shower will make it so much less embarrassing when they sing *Happy Birthday* to you tonight."

All I can do at this point is shake my head in horror because she's right. At least I'll know once they sing to me this nightmare of an evening will be ending.

Xavier stands and pulls out my now-dry chair for me. I sit, looking up at him sheepishly as he pushes me in and I say, "Thank you."

"Are you okay?" Xavier asks in his best-concerned voice while trying to hide his smile as he takes his seat.

"You're allowed to laugh, Xavier," I manage to say through the embarrassment. "Roxanne is content continuing to shatter my ego, so you might as well join in the fun at my expense."

He comes in close and whispers in my ear, "If it makes you feel any better, your hair looks hot in a ponytail. It reminds me of the day you ran into me on the running trail." He leans away and places his hand on my leg. "Joy, in the last month you ran into me on a running trail, you ran into me at your work, and now today, you managed to get water poured all over you in one of the most famous restaurants in the world. I am beginning to think this is the real Joy: uncoordinated, in a hurry all the time, and a tad clumsy. Which only makes me appreciate you more. I think it's endearing."

Christopher, who's been surprisingly quiet through this catastrophe, asks, "Can we add tonight as just one more reason we don't celebrate Joy's birthday?"

Instinctively, I throw the roll from my plate right at his head. His reflexes kick in just in time, and he manages to duck out of the way with a laugh. This action allows my roll to continue its travels through the restaurant, landing on a nearby table, which only draws more attention in our direction.

"I'll take that as a yes," he says with a chuckle, looking at Roxy and wiping imaginary sweat from his brow.

The guys ordered for us while I was in the restroom drying off, and as we wait for our dinner to arrive, the tension fades, replaced by a shared anticipation regarding whether the meals will live up to the hype surrounding this restaurant.

For my main course, I devour a pan-seared sea bass, which is an absolute triumph. The fish is cooked to perfection, and its skin is delectably crispy and golden.

Roxanne and I decide to share our meals, a daring move for such a fancy restaurant, but it allows us to experience the best of both dishes and we're not really ones to follow the rules of society. Roxanne and Xavier opted for the filet mignon, a succulent cut of tender beef cooked to their preference. Both are topped with a delicious cream sauce that adds richness to the dish.

The food is nothing short of perfection, and the service is impeccable. Our glasses are never empty, except for the one memorable moment when a server dumped seven glasses of water over my head, which will probably haunt me forever.

After dinner I grab my things from Roxanne's car and drive home with Xavier. The silence on the drive home so far is deafening. After how dinner played out, I'm not sure what to say. Childhood memories play through my mind of my grandparents taking me to the Sizzler Buffet and me thinking that it was a fancy dinner out. We continued the birthday tradition even after my grandpa passed. The last dinner I had with my grandma was at Sizzler for my twentieth birthday the day before she died. If they could've only seen tonight's dinner. They'd love Xavier, and they'd be so proud of the adult I've become, with the expectation of me taking out the passing waiter and wearing his entire tray of water.

"Thank you for tonight; it has been my most memorable birthday to date," I say and smile at him. "I'd love for you to stay with me tonight when we get back to my apartment?"

"Are you sure?" Xavier asks. "You've been quiet tonight. I assumed you weren't feeling well or just over everything tonight."

"I owe you an explanation," I say, surrendering to the truth. Before whatever this is between us goes any further, he deserves the truth. I've always kept guys at arm's length, hesitant to let them see the real me. My childhood is complicated and painful, something I've always kept hidden from others, with the exception of Roxanne. It's not something I enjoy reliving, so I don't share it with anyone.

I position myself so I can look at Xavier as he drives. Knowing he's preoccupied with driving allows me the freedom to have this conversation without having to maintain eye contact.

"Xavier, I don't celebrate my birthday. The last birthday I celebrated was my twentieth, the day before my grandma died. She and I went to Sizzler; it was our birthday tradition. We did it while my grandpa was alive and committed to doing it even after he died."

Xavier looks from the road for a quick second and asks, "Why didn't you tell me? I would've never forced a celebration on you if you had been honest with me."

I place my hand on his thigh to reassure him. "I didn't want to tell you. I was embarrassed. Do you know how hard it is to come to terms with the fact that you were born to two people who didn't want you, so you had to be taken in by your grandparents? Only for them to die when you still felt like a child. It's just a shitty reminder of who I am."

Glancing away from the road once more, he says, "Joy, you are so much more than the girl no one wanted the day you were born. Your parents are missing out on the most incredible person I've ever met. You're sweet and funny, and tonight, you've proven your clumsiness wasn't a fluke," he says with a chuckle.

Chapter 11

Xavier and I ride the elevator up to my apartment. I take his hand, needing to show him how much I appreciate him.

In a soft voice, I say, "Xavier, I loved tonight. It was one of the best birthdays I've ever had. You are one of the most thoughtful people I've ever met. I can't thank you enough for what you did." My voice trails off as I struggle to keep my emotions in check.

As we enter my apartment, darkness envelops us. I feel my way up and down the wall for the living room ceiling light. Finding the familiar shape of a switch, I flick it, and we're immediately surrounded by light and my familiar small but perfect one-bedroom apartment.

I take Xavier's hand once again, lead him to the couch, push him down, and lower myself between his legs. I take his suit shirt, untuck it, and start to unbutton it from the top down. "What are you doing?" he asks in a breathless voice.

Making my way from his shirt buttons to his belt, I say, "We've talked so much tonight. I want to do something else. Is that okay with you? I mean, it is my birthday and all."

"Fuck, Joy, um yeah, if you're feeling up to it after all the emotions of today."

I look up to him, and he lays his head back onto the couch cushions and surrenders his body to me. I finish removing his pants, then his boxer briefs and take his cock out and then stand. He lifts his head from the cushions and looks up to see me just as I reach around to the back of my dress and unzip it. I allow it to fall and pool around my feet. He slowly strokes his cock as he watches me unhook my black-lace bra and remove my matching black-lace panties to the floor, before stepping out of them and my dress.

"Joy, you're the sexiest fucking girl I've ever seen." His voice is low and throaty.

Without saying anything, I lower myself to my knees in front of him and remove his hand from his cock. I place my mouth to the tip of his dick and lap up the pre-cum that has already started to leak out due to his anticipation. I lick him up and down, paying particular attention to the large bulging vein that runs the entire length. He moans, and that gives me encouragement to take his entire cock in my mouth, moving slowly at first up and down only to quicken my pace. I take his balls in my hand and massage them as I continue my pace.

"Fuck, baby, you're killing me. It's your birthday, and I should be pleasuring you."

I moan, and the sensation on his dick pulls a gasp from him. He takes my hair, already in a ponytail, and wraps it around his fist, allowing him to take control of my speed, pulling me up and down on his cock. His motions quicken, and he thrusts his hips to get as far into my mouth as possible. I gag as he touches the back of my throat, tears filling my eyes. I refuse to stop, and I look up at him. Our eyes connect, mine watery and his full of desire. I give him a devilish smile as I pull him almost completely out of my mouth. That teasing only encourages his hip to thrusts back into me as he seeks out his orgasm.

"Baby, I can't hold back much longer. I need to come. Come and ride me. I want to finish inside you."

There is not a chance in hell I'm going to stop blowing him and not allow him to come in my mouth. I quicken my motion moving up and down, sucking deep into my mouth. The control of giving him a blowjob is empowering, and I have to taste him. My free hand goes to the base of his dick, and I wrap my hand around his him squeezing, making a tight fist around his cock. I twist and pump him as my sucking becomes harder and quicker.

"Joy. Fuck, I can't; I'm going to—" And then, with a loud groan, he explodes in my mouth, filling me with his warm release. He grabs onto my head and continues to fuck my mouth until he has completely emptied himself inside me. Once he comes down from his orgasm and relaxes into the couch, I lick him from base to tip, making sure to lap up all of him.

"Joy, that was—" He stops mid-sentence and crashes his lips onto mine. Not a second thought was given to the fact that he just came inside my mouth. His kiss is a sudden, passionate expression of raw desire and need.

Everything is replaced with this moment right here. I know as I move forward, my birthday will be forever altered by the overwhelming significance of today's events.

As the sunlight blinds me through my open curtains—another reminder of my forgetfulness—I shift in bed and moan. God, I hope no one could see Xavier and me last night. I throw my pillow over my head, only to realize I don't feel the weight of Xavier next to me. I quickly sit up and look around. No Xavier.

I yell from bed, "Xavier, are you here?"

"In the kitchen."

Forcing myself out of bed, I follow the aroma of coffee that leads down my hallway to a sexy man standing only in tight boxer briefs in my kitchen.

"Well, this is one way to wake up," I say with a little more pep in my voice.

"Good morning, beautiful," he says with a kiss to my forehead. "I have to meet Harper in an hour, but I'm taking you to an early dinner, let's say, four p.m. Does that work for you?"

"Does what part work for me? The part about you leaving first thing to meet Harper or dinner?"

"Dinner," he answers, his eyes narrowing and his jaw tightening in clear irritation.

"Both work perfectly," I say with a forced smile, showing him the carefree, no-conflict Joy that I show the world. The girl who prides herself on not rocking the boat as I do my best to make sure everyone around me is taken care of and happy, but on the inside, I'm fuming. How could any guy think it's okay to fuck me like he did last night and then sneak out the next morning to see his cousin… who I hate!

After Xavier showers and leaves to meet Harper, I fight the urge to text Roxy, which is successful for two hours max.

Me – He's an ass.

Roxanne – Good morning to you, too.

Me – It's late morning now, and Xavier just left to meet Harper.

Roxanne – Oh, the other woman.

Me – Shut up!

Roxanne – ...

Me – What do you mean...

Roxanne – Are you mad at Xavier for leaving to meet his cousin, or are you mad that today is the anniversary of your grandmother's death, and he's not there with you?

Me – Both

Roxanne – I expected you to lie, so I'm honestly at a loss for advice, but I will say they're best friends. Give it a rest already.

Me – I think Xavier and I are getting too close; maybe we need a break or to see other people.

Roxanne – Right on cue, you're falling for him, so you're going to push him away. AND, you're literally throwing a temper tantrum because he's with his cousin, and you think it's a good idea for him to see other girls who he can actually fuck?

Me – You're no help.

Roxanne – You're a mess.

Me – But you love me.

Roxanne – Yes, I do. Are you going to your grand-ma's grave today? Do you want me to come?

Me – No, I don't think I'm going. I'm going to have a me day.

Roxanne – Wow, this is new. But, if you change your mind, I'm here.

Once I'm done texting Roxanne, I send a quick text to Xavier because why wouldn't I sabotage the best thing that's ever happened to me on the anniversary of my grandmother's death?

Me – Hey, I got called into work today, so I don't think I can make dinner. Maybe tomorrow?

It's a lie, of course, but I need space to think. Xavier and I have been inseparable for the past month, and it's starting to feel suffocating. Maybe Roxanne has a point. Maybe the issue lies with me, not with him or Harper. I've always kept people at a comfortable distance to protect my heart, which I've never denied, but somehow, Xavier has managed to burrow under my skin, and it feels a little too much, too soon.

I put on some makeup, get dressed, and head in the direction of work. I didn't get called in, but it'll be nice to pass the time there and get my mind off Xavier for a bit.

"Why are you here?" Bryan asks.

"Nice to see you too," I reply a little too harshly.

"You work too much," he says.

"You know you're the only boss in the world that would complain about an employee working too much?"

"Maybe, but that doesn't change the fact that you do indeed work too much."

I just shake my head as I walk to my desk.

I've been at work for hours trying to busy myself and keep my mind off my grandma, Xavier, and how I'm fucking up my life one bad decision at a time. Nothing is helping my racing mind. I can't stop glancing at my phone, hoping for a reply from Xavier and hating myself for caring. With every peek, I grow more and more frustrated. I push my chair back with a bit more force than I expected, almost making me lose my footing and fall back with my chair, which of course only makes me more mad. I have to get out of here. I take a deep breath, right my chair back under my desk, grab my purse, then make my way out of the sales office.

As I walk out of the dealership, the cool, refreshing air greets my face. I take a deep, calming breath as I subconsciously head toward the back lot where all the employees park. As I approach my car, I look up and, sure enough, there's Xavier, dressed casually in dark denim jeans and a snug white golf-style shirt that clings to his biceps, effortlessly showcasing every perfect inch of his arms. He's leaning against my driver's door, arms crossed in front of his chest. "Are you ready for dinner?" he asks.

"What are you doing here?" I ask.

"Joy, you weren't scheduled to work today."

"No, but one of the guys needed time off for one of his kid's things."

He nods his head, clearly not buying my lie. "Are you going to tell me the truth about why you'd rather work today of all days than go to dinner with me?"

"It's been busy; they needed me," I say as I make a sweeping motion to show him the vast dealership where I work.

"Gotcha, but they're busy every day, and you still manage to take days off, and when you're, in fact, busy at work, you still manage to text me at least twenty times and call me once."

"You make me sound so clingy," I say, pouting sourly.

"I like you clingy, Joy," he says as he pushes himself away from his car, grabs my arms, and wraps them around his neck, forcing me to stand on my toes.

He then proceeds to wrap his arms around my waist. He's so warm and strong, and we're so close that his heart beats against my chest, which only means he can feel mine racing as if I just sprinted a quarter mile in under four minutes. After what feels like an eternity, I take a deep breath and allow myself to relax into his embrace.

"Please don't be jealous of mine and Harper's relationship. She's my cousin and one of the most important people in my life. I'd never come between you and Roxanne, and I expect the same respect from you."

"I'm sorry. I don't know why I'm so insecure about her. It's not usually who I am," I mummer into his muscular chest because he's right. He'd never ask me not to spend time with Roxanne, and if he were spending time with anyone other than Harper, I wouldn't care. Like at all! So, why do I let her get under my skin so bad?

He walks me to the passenger side of my car and opens the door for me. After he motions for me to get in, I slide into the passenger seat. He walks around, gets into the car, and starts to drive.

"Where are we going?" I ask.

"You'll see." He glances at me with soft, tender eyes, a smile playing on his lips.

"How was today?" I ask.

He continues to look at me and says, "Joy, I'm not doing this with you right now. I refuse to let you ruin this evening for us."

I hold up my hands in defense and say, "I was just trying to make conversation."

He nods and hums, "Mmm-hmm."

After driving for about fifteen minutes to a not-so-great part of town, we pull into a not-so-great parking lot. "What are we doing? Why are we stopping?"

"Look ahead." He motions ahead of us with a nod.

Huge white letters, all capitalized, sit on top of a rundown building flickering with the name SIZZLER. I sit in the passenger seat, stunned. My heart pounds in my chest as I wrestle to contain the overwhelming flood of emotions threatening to consume me. I take deep breaths, trying to compose myself. Tears sting my eyes, blurring the words on the sign just a few feet before me. Xavier opens my door and reaches in for my hand.

"My lady, I think I owe you a traditional birthday dinner."

Chapter 12

It's Roxanne's wedding day. I'm in the bridesmaid's room putting the final touches on my hair, getting ready to meet Roxy for a few pictures in the garden.

There's a knock on my door. "Come in, it's open," I shout, assuming it's the photographer here to fetch me.

The door opens and, in an instant, my heart stops. I immediately lose it, tears streaming down my face in torrents, an emotional flood that words can't even begin to describe.

"What are you doing here?" I manage to ask between sobs, my voice breaking.

"I wanted to surprise you." Roxanne's familiar calm voice.

"Well, you did a damn good job of that. You look beautiful, Roxanne." I choke out franticly, wiping away tears, desperately trying not to ruin my makeup. "Why are you here? we're supposed to be taking pictures in the garden soon."

"The wedding won't start without me, Joy," she says with a confident grin.

And that's my best friend. Confident, carefree, and the most amazing person I've ever met.

Roxanne is wearing an off-white, trumpet-style dress with elaborate beading throughout. It has a low V in the back, open sides, and plunging V at the bust. It's fitted through her hips, and covered in her veil; she looks like she just walked out of a children's fairy tale. Given her petite frame, she was able to buy her dress straight off the rack with a few simple alterations.

Roxanne and her dad make their way from the staging area in the garden where pictures were taken to the chapel. I'm already staged at the alter with Christopher and his best man who I've never met before today. I turn back when I hear the music start and catch a glimpse of Roxanne and her dad through the double doors. She looks beautiful, and I don't know if I've ever seen her look happier than she does in this moment. Roxanne takes her time making her way down the aisle, creating eagerness for all of us and anxiousness for Christopher.

Christopher's eyes glisten with unshed tears and shimmer with a mix of joy and love. Roxanne's father hands her off to him. I turn to wipe my face and try to save some of my makeup—again! Xavier and I share a prolonged and intense gaze. He nods, encouraging me to stay strong and keep it together.

Roxanne hands me her bouquet, and I hand her Christopher's ring. When our hands meet, she squeezes mine for a second longer than necessary and winks; I wink back and motion her attention back to Christopher. They exchange their vows, and before I realize what is happening, her sister is nudging me to walk back down the aisle because the ceremony has ended, and my best friend is officially married.

• • •

Xavier takes my hand and leads me to the dance floor after Roxanne and Chris finish their first dance.

"I'm a terrible dancer," I whisper into Xavier's ear.

He chuckles when he says, "Based on how clumsy you are in your daily life, Joy, that comes as no surprise to me." Then he pulls me close to his chest and moves us effortlessly across the dance floor.

As we dance, I take in the three hundred guests, laughing and enjoying the company of the bride and groom. Roxanne is engrossed in a conversation with her three cousins, and there's a familiar pain in my chest that I've tried to ignore for the last few weeks. It's not jealousy because I have too much appreciation for Roxanne's family to feel jealous. Maybe it's sadness knowing that I'll never have a day like this. My father will never walk me down the aisle. I don't have siblings to stand next to me when I exchange my vows, and it's another milestone that my grandma won't be able to experience with me. I only have Roxanne, and I think today is the day I've officially lost a considerable part of her to Christopher.

"Are you okay?" Xavier whispers in my ear. "As much as I'd like to think you're lost in our dance, knowing you, I don't think that's the case." He gently separates me away from his chest, looks directly at me, and says, "Talk to me, Joy. What's going through your overactive brain?"

"I wish I could answer that question with certainty, but I don't think I have the answer. I'm so happy for Roxanne, but there's a huge part of me that is experiencing a great deal of loss at the moment, and I feel extremely selfish for saying that aloud. What kind of person does that make me? I'm envious of watching my best friend, who I've known since childhood, get everything in life that she's ever wanted."

"The kind of person who has only experienced loss and abandonment." He pulls me back into him, and I rest my head on his shoulder. "Joy, Roxanne has been your one and only constant since childhood. It's okay to be scared that you may lose some of that connection."

Before I can say anything, the DJ comes over the loudspeaker and sings, "All my single ladies to the dance floor. It's time for the bouquet toss, and single men; I'd like you just off to the side so we can know what lucky guy will be taking home Roxanne's garter."

I cringe at the idea of some random guy catching Roxanne's sweaty garter.

I quickly say to Xavier, "Let's get off the floor before we're subjected to this stupid tradition."

"Wait, what?" he says, a frown consuming his face as I try to drag him off the dance floor, only for Roxanne to grab me by my arm then and drag me back onto the dance floor. She positions me smack dab in the middle of everyone, and then she proceeds to use her arms to separate those close enough to interfere with the bouquet landing in my arms.

"Roxanne, I'm not comfortable with this," I shout as she turns her back to us single ladies and looks to Christopher for guidance on exactly where she should aim her bouquet, so it is impossible for me to miss.

Before I have an opportunity to run, she hucks it over her shoulder, and it hits me straight on the side of my face like a bullet. I bend down, pick it up, and hold it, shaking my head in utter embarrassment.

Roxy shrieks as she jumps up and down. "Oh my God, I can't believe you caught it. It's fate."

I burry my face in my hands, this time more annoyed than embarrassed, and simply say what I always say to her, "Roxanne, I hate you."

She runs over to hug me and says, "Good thing I love you enough for the both of us."

Roxanne and Christopher leave after the cake is served for their week-long honeymoon in Hawaii. Xavier and I stay to help box up centerpieces table by table and deposit them into multiple family members' vehicles. Once that's completed, we're entrusted with gathering all the wedding gifts and safely driving them to Roxanne and Christopher's apartment. To say Xavier's Lexus is jammed packed with gifts doesn't even start to describe it. I'll officially be a pro at Tetris after tonight.

As we walk back into the reception hall after packing up Xavier's car, I ask Roxy's exhausted mom, "What else can I do before we leave?"

"Nothing, babe. There's plenty of family left to finish up here; take your handsome boyfriend home and enjoy what is left of this evening," she says, her face glowing from her makeup and so much pride in her eyes. But those three words, "*plenty of family*," are a harsh reminder of the unfortunate reality of my life. As much as Roxanne and her family have and will always show me love on some level, I'm genuinely not their family or ever will be. And, after a perfect evening like tonight, the truth strikes me harder than I could've ever anticipated.

Trying to sound unphased, I say, "Okay, we're heading out then."

Her mom hollers as we're almost out of the door. "I love you, Joy girl. I'm so glad you caught the bouquet," she says with a wink.

Looking at Xavier, I give him an apologetic smile. "I'm sorry for her. Subtlety isn't her thing."

Xavier puts his arm around my shoulder and pulls me close. "I'm glad you caught it too." And apparently, subtlety isn't his thing, either.

Trying to hide my smile, I ask, "Are you coming home with me?"

He grabs a handful of my ass in agreement, and shivers travel down my spine, lighting up every nerve ending until it reaches my toes. The way Xavier makes me feel is equally terrifying and exhilarating. The reaction of my body to his touch also thrills and terrifies me, leaving me feeling a mix of being scared, uncertain, and a little too vulnerable.

Chapter 13

I wake up to Xavier staring at me. "What the hell, Xavier? You scared the crap out of me."

"I'm starving," he says slowly for some dramatic effect. "I know it's early, but can we go eat?" he's practically begging me.

I look at my phone charging next to me and moan, "It's six am."

"And I'm starving."

"Yes, you made that clear already," I say, pulling myself from my very warm bed and grabbing a pair of leggings I find lying on the floor and a ripped-up concert T-shirt from my closet.

I brush my teeth and put my hair in a high ponytail. A high ponytail has been my go-to look since my birthday, knowing how much Xavier likes it.

Once I'm done, I tap my foot as if I'd been ready for hours and motion to my watch as Xavier finishes brushing his teeth.

"Can we walk to the café just on the corner? Between work and Roxanne's wedding, I haven't run in weeks."

"Did I mention I'm starving?" he says as he clutches his stomach.

"Okay, okay, we can drive," I chuckle before we make our way to my car in the parking garage.

When we get to the café, he orders scrambled eggs well done, sourdough toast, turkey sausage, and hashbrowns. I order pancakes, and then we split our meals in half. Well, maybe not fifty/fifty, but seventy/thirty, which is fine for me since I haven't been doing any cardio, and with my petite frame, pancakes add up fast.

"How do you feel after the wedding last night?" he asks as he shovels food into his mouth.

Laughing at him, I say, "It was great. Everything she wanted."

With his mouth still full of food, he says, "No, I didn't ask how Roxanne feels; I asked how you feel."

"Oh, I felt good, but now I'm just totally grossed out by the way you're eating," I say with a chuckle.

He smiles, takes a minute to swallow his food then continues, "What do you envision your wedding day to look like?"

Choking on my food, I cough and pound on my chest. "I've never given it much thought," I croak out around sips of water.

"Wait, what? What girl doesn't dream about her wedding day?"

"This girl," I admit. "I've never envisioned being married."

"Like you don't want to be married?" he asks, his fork paused midair for the first time since he got his breakfast.

"Not exactly; I've never imagined a guy staying around long enough to marry me?" I say as I move my fork through the syrup on my plate.

"Man, Joy, who hurt you so bad you can't imagine anyone wanting to marry you?"

I reply with the only answer that comes to my mind, "My parents."

"Your parents. Wait, I don't understand," he says, his brow furrowing in confusion. "What did your parents do? Have you never seen a happy married couple?"

"No, my grandparents were happy," I say matter-of-factly.

"Did they tell you no one would ever want to marry you?" he asks, his eyes probing mine for my reaction.

"No." My answer is dry and emotionless.

"Then what do you mean, Joy?"

"My parents never had to *say* anything to hurt me like they did. If the two people who are supposed to love you unconditionally don't, why would anyone else?" I say flatly because that's my truth. I'm not really sad about it anymore. It just is what it is.

"I hate that your parents made you feel like you're not enough."

I give him a half smile and say, "I do too."

Walking out of the restaurant, I step in gum. "Dammit," I exclaim.

"What's wrong?" Xavier asks.

"I just stepped in gum," I say as I fidget with my shoes, scuffing them on the sidewalk outside the restaurant.

Gracefully, Xavier swoops me into his arms, cradling my body against his.

"Okay, if I knew this would happen when I stepped in gum, I'd carry extra sticks and strategically place them whenever a handsome, strong man was around."

He shakes his head and smiles. "Any handsome man, or just this handsome man?"

Still distracted by my shoe, I casually answer, "I only have eyes for you, Xavier."

From across the street, someone shouts, "Xavier..." Then a little louder and more forceful, "*Xavier.*"

"Shit," Xavier murmurs under his breath. Then he waves across the street.

I look up from my shoe to see who it is, and to my dismay,

it's his cousin Harper-fucking-Atwood; and she's coming toward us from the other side of the street. If that wasn't bad enough—because trust me, it should be—she's dragging my ex-boyfriend by his hand.

And now it's my turn to murmur, "Shit" under my breath.

Xavier sets me down and steadies me while I continue to fuck with my shoe.

"Xavier!" Harper says, wrapping him in a hug. She looks at me and asks, "Is this why I haven't heard from you in the past few weeks?" Then she looks me up and down with a smile I can't quite make out.

"I just saw you last weekend, Harper." Xavier's voice is nervous, but I'm unsure why.

Harper is a beautiful blonde; mine is champagne. She is the complete opposite of me in every way. She is tall—almost six feet, while I'm short. She has a thin build—I guess we're similar there—but she has unmistakable piercing green eyes, and mine are blue. She has olive skin, mine is fair. She is quiet, well I guess I'm quiet too, so we're similar there too, but I'm sweet, well not her, but I am, and she's not. And I swear I sound like a child in my head right now.

"Harper..." Xavier stammers for a second then asks, "What are you guys doing here?"

I stay silent because Harper and Gabe are the last two people I ever need to converse with.

Gabe stammers, clearly as uncomfortable as Xavier, maybe even more, but he still manages to give me an obligatory, "Hi, Joy, how are you?"

I nod. "I'm good. Thanks for asking," is all I give him.

Harper looks between Xavier and me and says, "Wait, are you two together? Is Joy the girl you were telling me about last weekend? Why didn't you tell me it was Joy, *like this Joy...*"

She looks between Gabe and me, and I think that's when reality finally sets in for her.

It's funny how much can change in a year. I have a flashback of when Gabe and I were on our way out and ran into Harper and Xavier outside our apartment elevator. I immediately knew there was something between Gabe and Harper when they saw each other. Their chemistry is undeniable. So, standing here today with Xavier as my boyfriend and seeing the two of them together is very ironic. Looking at Xavier, I say, "This feels strangely familiar."

Xavier quickly says, "Well, we better go; Joy has to work today. Harper, I'll call you later." He pulls me along with him and we hurry away as if we're fleeing a crime scene.

"You better, because if you don't, I'll find you." She makes that weird gesture with her two fingers at her eye and then points to his eye. The gesture is creepy, but it's also very weird to see Harper actually being playful.

"That was uncomfortable," I say as we head to my car, parked just across the street from the restaurant.

"What part?" Xavier asks jokingly.

"All of it. But specifically, seeing them together and seeing her face when she saw us together. Did you not mention we were fucking when you left me on the anniversary of my grandma's death to meet her for breakfast last weekend?"

He stops and turns to me, clearly taken back by my shitty comment. "I can see how uncomfortable it must be to see them together, and I'm sure she's not thrilled seeing us together either. Only because under her harsh exterior, I know she feels a little responsible for your and Gabe's breakup. So, seeing you is a reminder of that."

"So, you didn't tell her about me."

He opens his mouth to answer, but I hold up my hand and

add, "Xavier, that wasn't a question. You care more about Harper's feelings than you do mine, and if you leaving me the other morning didn't drive that fact home, today definitely did."

"Do you think Harper loses sleep over you?"

I try to interrupt to answer him, but he mimics my action from seconds ago and holds his hand up. "Joy, that wasn't a question." He takes a calming breath and adds, "I need you to get over this Harper versus Joy bullshit. It's getting old, and it's completely unjustified. We argue about one thing and one thing only—Harper, and the worst part about this said argument is she shouldn't even be a factor in our relationship. So, to answer your question, no, I didn't tell her I left you to see her, because it's none of her business."

Chapter 14

Roxanne is finally home from her honeymoon, and we're meeting for drinks tonight after what feels like an eternity apart. Before she accepted Chris's proposal, she made him promise that he would support our girls' nights once a month.

I'm dressed in a tight black mini-dress that falls at my mid-thigh. I'm afraid if I were in high school and had to do the fingertip test, I wouldn't pass.

Hurrying out of the door because I'm *always* running late, who do I see at the elevator... Harper and Xavier. "Fuck my life," I say under my breath.

But to them, I say, "Hi. You both look fancy. Off to somewhere nice?"

"You could say that," Harper replies, giving me no clue as to where they're off to.

Harper is in a dress that leaves nothing to the imagination. It's short and sits just below her ass, and a low-cut V in the front exposes her entire flat, perfect mid-section down to her belly button. She has black spiked heels, which make her at least six feet tall. God, I hate this girl. She is the girl who walks into a room and instantly makes every other girl feel like her understudy. It's not just her beauty. It's her presence; I've never walked into a room and had every person stop to look at me. Xavier has black slim-fit pants, a tight black long-sleeve button-down, and black dress shoes. He looks as good as he smells. But with his all-black, he seems like he should be with me, not her.

Xavier leans over, kisses my cheek, and whispers, "You look smoking hot, baby."

"Thank you," I reply as my cheeks flush, which I'm sure is totally obvious thanks to my fair skin handed down by the two people who wanted nothing to do with me. But am I blushing from embarrassment or anger?

"Where are you off to tonight?" Xavier asks me.

"I'm meeting Roxy. She just got home from her honeymoon, and I'm dying to hear about it. We are trying to continue our girls' night once a month."

When I say this, Harper smiles. And I have no idea what the meaning behind it is.

Then she says, "Xavier told me all about the wedding when we were doing some planning for mine this week. It sounds like it was beautiful."

And I guess that was her way of breaking the news that she and Gabe are not only dating but getting married soon.

Skipping past that nugget of information, I ask again, "What about you guys? Where are you off to looking so amazing?"

Harper puts her arm through Xavier's as if to claim him.

Again, I want to say, *'Hi, Harper, I've been fucking your cousin, and no matter how much you try to claim him, I've had him, and I've fucked your boyfriend Gabe too… So that's two for Joy and one for Harper.'* But I don't because girls like me don't say things like that to girls like Harper.

Harper says, "It's one of my co-worker's birthdays, so we're all celebrating with him tonight." Her tone is so excited that it makes it hard for me even to look at her, let alone read her. Why do I hate her so much? Why didn't Xavier tell me he had plans with her tonight? Maybe because I've been avoiding him since breakfast a few days ago. How does she feel about Xavier and me dating? If she were happy about it, wouldn't she make more effort with me? Is she waiting for me to make more of an effort with her? Should I have lied and said I was going on a date to get in Xavier's head like he and Harper are mine?

Irritated, I muster in the perkiest voice, "Well, I'm going to take the stairs. I can't be late because this elevator has been taking too long. Have a great time tonight."

Xavier moves away from Harper, pulls me close to him, and whispers in my ear, "The party is here in your building. I can wait for you to come home and stay with you tonight. I feel like you've been avoiding me. I'd love to be the person to peel that dress off you tonight."

I look from him to Harper, standing there casually looking at her phone, and reply, "No, you have fun tonight with Harper. I'll call you tomorrow." Without looking back, I run to the stairs. Once I'm safe inside the stairwell, and the door shuts behind me, I lean against the wall and try to control my breathing—not because of running four feet, but because of the panic attack I feel bubbling up inside my chest.

Patting tears from my cheeks and fanning my eyes, I do everything I can to save my mascara and foundation. My cell vibrates in my hand. Xavier shows up on my screen. I hit *Decline* and stuff my phone into my small clutch.

Once in the Uber, I pull out my phone to FaceTime Roxanne, as we always do, and I realize I have five missed calls from Xavier.

I ignore his calls and call Roxanne instead. "I'm in my Uber, are you?"

"Yes," she answers perfect time... "Hey, you okay?" she asks.

"No, but I'll explain when we're together." I look at my watch. "Three minutes for me, how about you?"

"Two minutes," she answers.

We sit there in silence for the remaining three minutes of my ride.

Once inside, we quickly order drinks. "Spill," Roxy demands.

"When leaving my apartment, I ran into Harper and Xavier."

Roxy wrinkles her forehead and chuckles. "No one has worse luck than you."

"I know, right!" I exclaim.

"So, what are they doing?"

"She said something like they were going to a co-worker's party. Hell, I don't remember. I'm not sure I was even listening. It was more like an out-of-body experience." I bury my face in my hands. Then whine, "Why does she get under my skin? All she did was smile when I said you and I were meeting. I wasn't even talking to her; I was talking to Xavier. Oh, and she made it a point to tell me she and Xavier are planning her wedding. Oh, I wonder who she's marrying."

"Gabe?" Roxy asks.

"Yes, Gabe!" I whisper shout. "Who else would she marry?"

"And, OMG, the audacity of her to smile at you," Roxy says sarcastically with her hand over her heart.

I hit my hands on the table, lean toward Roxanne, and say in a frustrated tone, "This is all you have to say. 'I can't believe she smiled at you'. What about the part where she and Gabe are getting married after like eight months of dating? Who gets engaged after eight months?"

Roxanne raises her hand, cutting off my rant.

"What?" I ask.

"Who cares if they got engaged after eight months? The only person who would care that someone is getting married is someone who isn't over said ex. And we all know you're over your ex, right? And besides, when you know, you know."

"Stop talking in code. I don't even know what you just said. And yes, eight months is too soon," I argue.

"Let's agree to disagree on that one," Roxanne says as she sips her drink. "Can I ask a question without you throwing your drink in my face?"

I nod at her, giving her permission to speak safely.

"Have you ever considered that Harper isn't your problem, that maybe you're your problem?"

"Whose side are you on?" I interrupt.

"I think I'm on Xavier's side, honestly. Come on, you said it yourself—she smiled at you, for Christ's sake. You're not mad at Gabe, or at least you weren't when you broke up, so why are you blaming her and not him? Have you considered maybe she avoided you because she felt bad for you? I don't know, Joy, if you don't change something, you're going to push Xavier away like you do everyone else in your life, and Harper will not only have Gabe, but she'll have Xavier too."

I growl way too loud for our small bistro table, which draws attention from neighboring tables. I give everyone looking at me an apologetic smile and realize I have serious issues that I need to deal with. Xavier was right when we were leaving breakfast. There is no way Harper loses sleep over me, so why am I over her?

"Rox, as much as I'd like to throw my drink at you and disagree, I don't think I can."

"I know," she interrupts, sitting up taller.

"Harper didn't steal Gabe," I continue.

"I know," she interrupts again.

"He left as a willing participant."

"I know."

"If you don't stop."

She makes a motion, zipping her lips closed.

"I can't be mad at her for the breakup. I can hate her for being a bitch, but not for Gabe."

"Is she really a bitch?" Roxanne asks, her face set in a serious expression, her eyes intense and focused on me as waits for me to answer.

"Well, I wouldn't know because she's never said more than ten words to me."

"So, she's quiet, reserved, shy, dare I say cautious, but 'bitch' you haven't proven to me."

I shrug, and she continues casually as she swirls her drink around her glass, "So, what's next?"

"Easy, I avoid Xavier forever," I say only half joking.

Roxanne furrows her brows and says, "Um, that isn't the solution I was looking for."

"He's too nice of a guy not to apologize for what happened tonight. It's up to me to stay strong and clear that I refuse to be second best to anyone, and that's how he made me feel tonight." I look down at my glass, then up at Roxy, and say, "Xavier didn't tell Harper I was the girl he was dating. Do you know how that made me feel when she said that?"

"Like it did when you ran into your dad's friends, and they had no idea you were his daughter?"

"Yeah, a little like that," I reply.

"But what you're missing is Xavier asked to spend the night with you after the party in front of Harper, so why are you pushing him away?"

"I don't know. Maybe I'm scared of getting hurt. Maybe I'm scared of not being enough or being too much."

"You need to confront these fears before you let the best guy you've ever dated slip away. If you lose him, you'll have no one to blame but yourself—not Harper, not Gabe, not Xavier—just lonely, self-doubting Joy."

"I never even asked about your honeymoon. I completely highjacked fun night and ruined it."

"My honeymoon was full of beach, waves and sex. There's not much more to tell unless you want the dirty details."

Shaking my head, I say, "Nope, I think you've shared enough."

I raise my hand to get our server's attention. "Can we get two more drinks?" I'm going to need it when she goes into *dirty details,* even though I said I didn't want them. She will share them.

Chapter 15

There's relentless banging in my head. I groan and press my pillow over my ears, hoping to drown out the throbbing but it's no use. Reluctantly, I start to get up, planning to take aspirin to stop the ache, when it finally registers – it's not my head that's banging, but my front door.

Walking to the door, I hold my head and yell, "Stop banging! I'm coming already!" I try to open the door, but I do not have the energy, and it's more of a slow peek around.

"Ugh, Xavier, what are you doing here so early?" When I try to speak, I sound like I've been smoking two packs of unfiltered cigarettes my entire life. I don't allow him to answer before I turn around and flop myself onto my couch, leaving the door open for him to either come in or go. I could care less at this very hungover minute in my life.

"You, okay?" He's genuinely concerned. Of course he's concerned about me because he's freaking perfect.

"I'll be fine after I throw up, shower, and eat. In that order," I say still in a really unattractive and very raspy voice.

"What can I do?" he asks.

"You can leave me to die alone," I answer.

"I'm not leaving, Joy."

"Of course you're not," I say under my breath just as a bout of nausea hits me. I jump up from my couch, knowing I won't make it to the bathroom down the hall. I run into the kitchen and vomit into my kitchen sink. I take one quick moment to thank my grandma for forcing me never to leave the house with dirty dishes in the sink, or this would've been much worse.

I turn on the water and garbage disposal, look at Xavier, then say, "I'm going to shower. I'll be back in a few."

After I brush my teeth and shower, I sit down on my bed to put my clothes on. I sit motionless for a minute, still wrestling with the ocean of alcohol in my stomach. I grab my blanket and tell myself I'll just lie down for a minute.

Opening my eyes, I realize the lighting is different from when I closed my eyes. It's dim with a bit of an orange hue throughout my apartment. I grab my phone, but it's not beside me, nor am I in the living room. I sit up in my T-shirt and panties, trying to get my bearings. I'm not wearing what I slept in, and my hair is wet. Squinting, I look at my bedside clock and shout, "Seven pm. Crap, I slept the entire day away." I bury my head into my pillow and moan.

"How do you feel?" a voice comes from my bedroom doorway, along with the most amazing smell of food—real food.

"What smells so good?" I ask, still with a raspy voice.

"Chicken parmesan and garlic bread," he answers.

"It smells like heaven." I get up, and the rush to my head is almost unbearable. I sit back down, put my head into my hands, and moan.

"You two must have had a great time last night if your hangover indicates how things went," he says, sounding a little bit more irritated now than concerned now.

"Yeah, we drank both our combined weight in tequila shots

last night," I say as I slowly get up and take some headache medicine from my nightstand that I must've forgotten to take last night, and down it with a bottle of water.

"I feel like shit, and I feel even worse knowing I've wasted my entire day off," I say, walking past Xavier into the living room to get my phone to see what I've missed today. Nothing. No texts, no missed calls, so I shoot a text to Roxy.

Me – You alive?

Rox – No, you're a terrible friend, and I'll never forgive you.

Me – Yeah, me too. See you tomorrow at work. Xx

Rox – If I don't die today.

Me – You won't die today unless Christopher is so mad at us, he's going to kill you. Make sure he knows the spouse is always the first suspect. Maybe that'll deter him.

Rox – You know we called him at two in the morning to pick us up, and he did, and he had to drag us away from a bachelor party that you insisted you were going with, and then you threw up in his car. He says you owe him a new car.

Me – Shit. Tell him I'm sorry and he can have mine.

Rox – I have to get back to sleep.

I put my phone on the counter. "She's as bad as I am," I tell Xavier as he sets the table. "So, what is all this?" I ask him.

"It's a truce," he says, avoiding eye contact and nervously scratching the back of his neck.

"For what?" I ask, knowing I'm the one who owes him an apology, not the other way around.

"Listen, Joy, last night in the hallway was…"

I interrupt, "I'm sorry. It was uncomfortable, and it's my fault."

He continues, "It's complicated to be stuck between Harper and you," he admits.

"Xavier, you are not stuck. I think it just has to be either you and her or you and I. We clearly don't work when it's Harper, Xavier and Joy. And I know how much she means to you."

"Joy, do you honestly think when I showed up at your dealership to buy a car, it was because Harper would force me to buy a car I didn't want?"

He shakes his head and continues, "Choosing a car my cousin and her fiancé don't sell wasn't an accident. It was a deliberate move on my part so I could run into you again, which you facilitated perfectly, and the rest is history." He moves toward me in the kitchen, and my stomach turns like a washing machine.

I'm still angry with myself, and there's a big part of me that feels like maybe we'll be better off not together, but it feels so right when he's close to me; I don't know if I want to fight him anymore.

He places his hands on my hips and hoists me onto the countertop. The granite is cold and a shock to my system, but it only steals my attention for a few seconds until it warms with my body heat. Xavier closes the distance between us, and the only space is filled with his clean scent. He takes each of my legs, wraps them around his waist, and pulls me closer to him. His erection presses against my pussy, and need pulses through me. Xavier takes my head in his hands and kisses me. Not a hard kiss like he usually gives me, but a soft and meaningful kiss. He whispers in my mouth, "I'm not letting you push me away, Joy."

Before I can say anything, he slowly drops to his knees and pushes my panties to one side. My mind races with a million distracting thoughts. Thank God I showered this morning. Do I taste like lingering alcohol? Even worse, do I taste like vomit? Did I kiss any of those guys last night? Oh God, how do I make my mind stop? How can I feel like a human again?

It takes one swipe of his tongue between the lips of my pussy and my entire body flinches with pleasure.

"Touch yourself, let me see how you work that sweet pussy when I'm not here to take care of you."

His words make my cheeks flush. No man has ever asked me to touch myself, and the thought makes me tingle with desire. I take one hand off the counter, not allowing my gaze to leave his, and gently slide my fingers between my folds, using my own wetness as lube. I rub small circles around my clit and place one finger inside me. This draws an involuntary moan from my throat, which causes Xavier to grow even more determined in his quest to pleasure me.

He pulls my finger from inside me and sucks it into his mouth. "You taste so good."

Then he takes my hand and places my finger in my mouth so I can taste me and him on my finger. Then guides it back down to my clit as he starts to fuck me with his tongue. I stop rubbing my clit to watch him and the momentary pause makes him look up to me and say, "I didn't say stop rubbing your clit, baby."

So I continue rubbing myself with small, languid circles.

He continues to eat me, alternating between gentle licks with his tongue on my clit and quick flicks as his tongue and my finger fight for power.

"Stroke yourself while you eat me. I need to see you," I say breathlessly.

He takes down his pants and boxer briefs just enough to free his cock all without breaking eye contact and without stopping his assault on my pussy, and I don't think I've ever seen anything so hot.

He takes one of his hands and strokes himself from his base to his head while he pushes two fingers into me. "Don't stop working that clit baby. And I won't stop working my cock for you."

"Xavier," I say, throwing my head back, which only motivates his relentless pursuit of pleasuring me.

He moans against my pussy, which encourages my cresting orgasm. I shamelessly drive my hips toward him and open my legs wider to allow him better access to my pussy. I grab his head with my free hand, entangle my fingers in his hair, and pull him into me, and right now, in this moment, I don't want to ever let him go.

"Oh God, Xavier, I'm right there; please don't stop," I scream, legs spread on my counter, my hands holding onto his hair as pleasure racks my body.

Looking up at me, Xavier says, "Don't hold back, baby, come all over my face. I want to taste all of you."

I come immediately.

Chapter 16

Six am alarms suck. I roll over and grab my phone to turn off my alarm and feel Xavier's arm reach around me to pull my body back into his.

"I have to go to work," I moan. "And so do you."

"Can't we be late?" he begs. "Just one more time."

We continued to have sex throughout the night last night, which I'm now convinced is the best cure for a wicked hangover. We didn't talk about Saturday other than his apology, which he didn't owe me, and at this point I'm not sure I even want to talk about it. I just want to be able to let it go and enjoy what's lying beside me without my wicked past blowing this to smithereens.

"Gabe's birthday is in two weeks; Harper is having a big party. Will you come and be my plus one, pleaseeeee?" he begs with his hands folded in front of him like a toddler begging for candy.

"Um, as much as I'd love to spend the evening with you as a plus one, I'd rather drown in the ocean to my death than spend a night partying with Harper at my ex-boyfriend's birthday," I say, running out of breath from my very long run-on sentence.

He laughs, which is a relief because I sort of regret saying that out loud.

"First, can we stop referring to my cousin's fiancé as your ex-boyfriend and just call him Gabe already? This will help both you and I move past what once was. And second, she's not a bad person. She wants to get to know you. If she's willing to try, I need you to be willing to try. Please, Joy, you'll come to learn that she's pretty amazing," he says, begging still.

Why is he so protective of her? "Can I ask you a question without offending you?" I don't wait for him to answer. "What do the two of you have in common other than blood? You're so warm and welcoming, and she's such a…" I pause, think better of what I'm about to say, and then say, "She's so cold."

Xavier says, "I wouldn't say she's cold; she's reserved and an introvert."

That makes me laugh out loud. "An introvert?" I question with a furrowed brow.

"Joy, she doesn't care to have friends, which is foreign to me, but with her past, I get it for her. Harper is actually very loving and is a ton of fun. But until you get to know her, you'd never think so. I think she does it to protect her heart. I think I've already told you this."

Everything Xavier says makes sense to me, but I cannot put Harper's name on the top of a page and those words below it to describe her. It just doesn't make sense.

Trying to steer the conversation away from Harper because that is what I do, I ask, "Where is Gabe's party tonight?" The last thing I care about is where his party is. Still, I desperately need to change the subject before this goes down a destructive path, and before he can even answer, I blurt out, "Shit, I have to get up and get ready for work; we've been lying here for thirty minutes. I'm going to be late to work if I don't hurry."

"Oh, Xavier, before I forget," I say, rushing out of bed and into the bathroom.

"Yeah," he hollers at me.

"I've shared a lot about my childhood and growing up—things I never shared with Gabe or anyone other than Roxanne. I'm still unsure why I felt comfortable sharing those things with you in such a short time. I know you and Harper are close, but I'd prefer the things I share with you stay between us only."

"I get it. I would never share your secrets. It's not my story to tell."

Chapter 17

y phone vibrates in my pocket.

Xavier – Busy for dinner?

Me – I was holding out for this very handsome guy who frequents my apartment building often. Can I get a raincheck?

Xavier – ha ha ha. See you at seven.

Me – I'm looking forward to it.

Xavier has been very attentive this week—texts, calls, and dinners almost every night. I'm sure he's trying to convince me to go with him to Gabe's birthday party this weekend. His being with me this week means he and Harper haven't been hanging out, and I'm sure if she weren't so busy with party planning, it would be sending her into a tailspin.

Opening my door to Xavier never gets old. He smells so good, manly with a hint of pine. He's dressed in slim-fit dark-blue denim pants and a short-sleeved button-down shirt that shows off his muscular arms, making his sky-blue eyes pop against his olive skin and dark blond hair. He's perfection in all the ways possible. His eyes burn a hole in my soul as he looks me up and down. His stare makes me feel underdressed. I'm wearing a tight purple dress with a low V that shows just a bit of cleavage. I have black heels on with clasps high around my ankles. Feeling uncomfortable, I ask, "Is this okay?" trying to break his stare.

"Yes, you look radiant."

"Radiant," I say with a chuckle.

"What?" he asks, as his shoulders slump in defeat.

"Who says radiant anymore?" I laugh.

"You look beautiful, hot, vibrant, and amazing. Yes, you look amazing; you are the winner. Now, can we do this before I mess up again?" His tone is eager with a hint of desire.

"Do you want to come in, or do we need to leave for dinner right away?" I ask with an unsure voice, and I don't know what changed to make me so nervous tonight. Was it his comment about being the winner? Is that his way of telling me I'm as important to him as Harper, or maybe if I'm lucky, more important? Or is it the way he smells or the way he looks? No, it's not. I think it's how he makes me feel when he looks at me. It's scary, much scarier than any other guy I've ever dated.

"We have time. I made sure to get here early."

I grab water and a beer, set them on the table, then plop down on the couch next to him. I look over to him to ask where we're going for dinner, and that's all it takes. He lifts me off the couch, cradles me in his arms, then carries me to my bedroom.

"Xavier, what are you doing?" My voice is breathless.

"What does it look like I'm doing?" His eyes burn into

me, revealing his deepest desires and unwavering passion. He adds, "I'm taking my girlfriend to her bedroom so I can make love to her."

My breath hitches, and I have to fight back the flood of emotions that hit me. He's going to make love to me; he's never used that term with me before. Our sex life is off the charts, but it's just that—sex: hot, sweaty, dirty, earth-shattering sex. We've never made love before.

"Xavier," I say in a whisper.

He looks at me again, and I feel an uncomfortable ache in my chest. "Please don't ever leave me.'

His expression softens, his voice gentle yet firm. "I won't, I promise. You belong to me now."

He places me on the edge of my bed; I take his hips in my hands and pull him closer to me. I undo his belt and jeans and watch them fall off his hips. He steps out of them, leaving his boxers on, and straddles my legs, trying to move closer to me, but I shake my hand and gesture at his boxers. "This won't do, boyfriend. I need these off. I need to see your cock."

He slowly pushes them down and steps out of them, before kissing my cleavage, where my dress doesn't cover, and says, "I've been wanting to kiss here since you opened your front door."

He pushes me back onto my bed so I'm lying flat on my back, my legs dangling off the edge still. Then he continues his journey down my chest; he kisses me lower and says, "And here." He moves the fabric of my dress, exposing my nipple. Looking up at me, he says in a strangled voice, "Especially here."

With every kiss, his cock grows harder and harder. Between his tongue teasing my nipples and his cock grazing every part of my body as he moves, lust flows through my veins like fire.

I need him right now like I have never needed anyone. No matter how hard I try, I can't get him close enough to me. I don't know what about him makes me feel like this, but no one has ever made me feel this alive or this possessive.

He lowers to his knees on the floor between my legs, grabs my thighs, and pulls me to his face. He kisses my left inner thigh, and then, not to leave out my right, he moves on to that one. With every kiss, he makes me wetter and wetter.

"You're glistening for me already, baby," he teases, and I'm not sure how much of his teasing I can take.

I sit up and slide off my bed onto my bedroom floor so we're both on our knees now. I position myself so I can stroke his cock while he continues to tease my body. He lets out a soft moan when I fist him in my right hand and slowly stroke him from base to tip.

He kisses my lips. "Can you taste yourself, baby? You taste like candy."

Getting lost in our kiss, I say, "Yes" in a breathless voice.

Our kiss grows more and more intense, all the while he is caressing my swollen and pleading clit. I try to keep pace and stroke his long hard cock, but I find myself getting lost in our kiss and the pleasure of him switching between fingering me and caressing my clit.

I can't take much more, so I whisper, "Fuck me, Xavier, before I come on your fingers. I want to come on your dick and feel your cum drip down my thighs all night."

He flips me around, pushes my face into the mattress, and rises to a standing position. He teases my entrance with his tip as he says, "Tell me if it's too much." He pauses momentarily every few inches to test how much of him I can take in this position. Once I'm accustomed to his size, he pushes himself all the way in, and oh my god, I can't stop the scream that comes from my mouth. He feels so fucking big and so fucking good.

He leans over me and whispers in my ear, "Are you okay?"

"Oh god, yes, don't you dare fucking stop." My words are muffed by the mattress.

"Oh, does my dirty girl like it when I pound into her cunt from behind?" he says.

I moan in response to his question.

"Fuck," he growls. He slows his pace for a few short seconds, pushing so deep into me that my ass stops his forward motion. He spreads my ass cheeks to allow himself to drive into me an inch or so more.

"Too much?" he asks.

"No, please don't stop, Xavier," I reply.

Slap. My ass is stinging and the feeling could make me orgasm alone.

"Again," I plead, and within a second, *slap* and another.

"I'm going to come, Xavier. Don't stop." He gives me one last slap and then reaches around to the front of me and rubs my clit with the softest amount of pleasure. The contrast of sensation coursing through my body is sensory overload. The pain of him slapping my ass, the pleasure of his cock filling me and the soft gentleness of his thumb rubbing circles on my clit, has me on the brink of the most intense orgasm I've ever experienced.

I scream, "Oh god, don't stop, Xavier. I'm going to come. Please don't stop."

He continues to pound into me from behind, and my orgasm reaches its peak, my body clenching around his cock.

I hear him moan, "Oh Fuck, Joy." He drives into me harder and harder as I grip my comforter in my hands to keep me in place. He is on the cusp of his own orgasm, and this is all too much for him. His breath quickens as he thrusts in and out of my dripping pussy. His body convulses as he comes inside me with one final thrust.

He doesn't pull out immediately but rests his upper body on my back, and we lay there for a few minutes, breathing as if we've both been running a marathon.

Once he catches his breath, he pulls out of me, grabs my hand, and together we retreat to my bathroom, which is fortunately attached to my bedroom. He turns on my shower to let it warm up and stares at me. My cheeks warm with his stare and I struggle not to say anything. Silence makes me more uncomfortable at this moment than ever before in my life.

"Should we get in?" I nervously ask, my fingers fiddling with my shower door handle as I glance up at him.

We both enter my not-huge shower, touching no matter what direction we turn. I'd say it's more comical than sexy, but I'm just enjoying being this close to him, watching the water cascade down his body, and the suds from my shampoo down his chest is enough to make me wet all over again. He catches me staring at him, and that's all it takes for him to lift me and wrap my legs around his waist. He uses the shower wall and his body weight to hold me up. I do everything I can to ignore how cold the tile is on my back, but as he inserts his stiff cock into me, I quickly forget about anything not related to him fucking me for a second time in less than thirty minutes.

He looks at me in my eyes as if he's trying to pull something out of me. His gaze forces me to look away, and he says, "No, look at me. I want to see your face when I come in you. Last time, I only got to see your back; this time, I want to see your pleasure reflected in your eyes."

Then he crashes his mouth on mine with so much force I get lost in him. This man can do whatever he wants to my body, and I won't protest. His cock feels perfect inside me, I don't want this to end.

I move my hips seeking more pleasure as he pounds into me. The only thing I hear is his balls slapping against my thighs and the sound of him groaning in my ear. I know he's close by the way his breathing picks up. He pinches my nipple between his fingers, and it sends a ping of electricity straight to my swollen clit.

With a throaty growl he says, "I'm close baby."

I hold onto his broad shoulders bracing myself as he fucks me into oblivion with brute so much force as he chases his release. He sucks my nipple into his mouth, and the sensation stirs an orgasm I feel with all my soul. "Don't stop, Xavier. I'm ready to come. Don't stop," I beg as my orgasm rips through me. *I thought the last orgasm was the best and now this... How is this even possible?*

My screams of pleasure were clearly all he needed to send him over the edge as he comes inside me. He grabs my wet hair and pulls my head into his chest as he comes down from his orgasm.

Sex with this man never disappoints, but making love to him is an experience beyond words. What just happened between us transcends mere physical pleasure. Every touch, every kiss, every thrust leaves me burdened with vulnerability and fear that terrifies me. What is growing between us is unlike anything I've known.

• • •

To deny that I'm falling in love with Xavier would not only be a lie but also a denial of my reality. He is the most attentive partner I've ever had. I have never felt so satisfied, satisfied in all the sexual ways, yes, but satisfied in this moment lying here in bed next to him. He's sleeping, and the sheets are pooled at his waist. I'm on my side, just basking in his presence. He's so comfortable in his skin, one of his most attractive things. Don't get me wrong, his six-pack is no eyesore either. This man is perfection, and it scares me as well.

Xavier stirs and opens his eyes. "Good morning," he says in a deep, sleepy voice that takes my breath away again.

I swear I can wake next to this man for the rest of my life and be happy.

"Good morning," I offer back in a relaxed, pleased voice.

"I'm sorry we skipped dinner last night."

"I'm not," I retort honestly because if I had to choose sex with this man or a fancy dinner, I'd choose him every day.

"What's on your mind?" he asks.

How does he know something is on my mind? He just opened his eyes thirty seconds ago. Does he know I've been staring at him?

"Nothing," I lie.

"You have a terrible poker face, Joy. What's on your mind?" he repeats.

"Honestly, I feel like there's an invisible weight on my shoulders due to the party this weekend, and although I'm not looking forward to going, you asked me to make an effort, so I will for you. And, if I'm being frank with myself, although Harper has not given me any reason to like her. She also hasn't given me any reason not to like her. Now I'm worried she won't like me, and I have no idea how I arrived here. A month ago, I disliked her for all the reasons I concocted in my head, none of which needed to be factual, but now that you're involved, I'm worried she won't like me, and you'll choose her over me. It's not like I can ask you not to speak to her," I say, trying to make what I just said make sense.

"Are you asking me not to speak to her? How old are we?"

That's a rhetorical question, so I don't answer.

"Harper and I are family. You get that right? Like blood." His jaw twitches, and I know he's upset. "We share a very long history, Joy, some of which you're unaware of."

Feeling shame creep in, I say, "I know, I'm sorry I'm being ridiculous. She brings out the worst in me."

"Joy, this is a one-sided battle, you get that right? Harper isn't your enemy. You are. I told you this once before: she's not a bad person. She's quiet, a loner, and she doesn't apologize for who she is."

Xavier throws the sheets back and hurries out of bed. He looks around the room for his discarded clothes, and panic takes over my body. I rush over to where he's standing naked and grab his arms, making him pause.

"When it comes to Harper, you make me feel second best." My voice is softer now for fear of driving him away. I continue, "You always defend her, and I don't like it. Do you defend me to her?" I say as I press my forehead to his chest.

"No, Joy, I don't! Do you know why? Because she doesn't make me. She has never spoken one ill word about you. Why can't you believe me?" He lifts my face to look at him. "Fuck, Joy, I'm sorry if you feel like I choose Harper over you; it's not like that at all. I wish you would've said something to me. I've been defending Harper my entire life. It's muscle memory. It's all I've ever done; it's all I know. But when it comes to choosing between the two of you. I don't want to. She's, my cousin. I love her. You're my girlfriend. I love you."

My gaze falls to the floor, but he lifts my head again, looks into my eyes, and says, "Joy, I love you."

Not knowing what to say, I nervously say, "Can we just

forget about the last five minutes?"

"What part?" he asks. "The part that you asked me to disown my cousin or the part I told you I love you, and you freaked out."

"Yes, yes. All of that," I say panicked.

Chapter 18

My phone rings, and the name on my screen makes me freeze. "Shit," I say under my breath; my heart is thundering in my chest and I don't know what to do. I can't avoid her forever, but I didn't think she'd call so soon. I saved her number to my contacts so she couldn't catch me off guard. But she's still managed to tip my world off its axis.

I wouldn't say I like confrontation. I avoid it at all costs, but she'd starve without it.

A voicemail alert appears on my home screen; I hit play and put the phone up to my ear.

"What the fuck, Joy? You can't keep him from me, and why would you even make him choose? I don't care what is happening with you, but your insecurities are not my problem. Stop dodging me and call me back."

"Okay," I say out loud. "That was interesting." Oh God, what if she comes to my apartment? I can't avoid her forever.

My phone vibrates with a text almost instantly.

Harper - *Oh, and everyone says your personality is indicative of your name. I'm calling bullshit, Joy. You're a broken mess just like the rest of us. YOU WON'T WIN.*

Not knowing what to do, I do the only thing that comes

naturally: run to Roxanne.

"Hey, girl, what's new?" Roxy asks.

"I think I fucked up."

She giggles. "You?" in her fake sweet southern accent.

"Rox, I'm serious," I say.

"What did you do this time?" she asks.

"I hinted to Xavier that I didn't want him to hang out with Harper."

"Ohhhhh," she says in her super-soft voice that she reserves for 'oh shit' moments like this.

"And how did that go over? What did he say when you requested that he break up with his *family* for a girl he just met a few months ago?"

"He said that," I say, frantic.

"He said what?"

"He said, what you said. About breaking up with family for a girl he just met. Well, he didn't say it exactly like that, but yeah, close enough." Nothing I'm saying is even making sense at this point.

"Yeah… probably not one of your finest requests," she says as if I was unaware of what I did.

"Did I mention she just called and yelled at me?"

"Shit, what did she say?"

"Cliff notes— That I can't keep him from her, and I know she's right."

"What did you say?"

"Nothing," I yell. "I let her go to voicemail. You know me, Roxy, I can't do this with her. She'll eat me alive. Why do I let her get to me? Why does she get under my skin?"

"Because she's everything you're not. I'm not saying she's better or worse than you, Joy, so don't go down some dark path. I'm saying facts are facts." She lowers her voice, "And

Gabe chose her, not you, and if push comes to shove, you know Xavier will too, so you're trying to test him, knowing you'll never win. This is a form of self-sabotage."

Everything she said is correct, and Roxanne is the only person who would be this brutally honest with me, and I love her for it. I assume that's why Harper loves Xavier as much as she does. We all need that one person who will love us through our mistakes.

"Should I call him?" I ask.

"Let him call you; he may need to catch his breath."

"Maybe you're right," I agree.

"Oh wait, before we hang up," she says quickly.

"What's up?" I ask.

"Maybe you can try with Harper?"

"Is that a question or a demand?"

"Maybe both?" she says in a tone that is more of a question than a demand.

Chapter 19

There's a knock on my door, and I reluctantly leave my balcony to answer it. As I open the door, my breath catches when I see Xavier standing there with his warm, familiar smile.

"Hey, can I come in?" Xavier asks.

"Sure," I say, moving to the side so he can enter.

"Can we talk?" he asks.

Fuck… fuck, fuck. Those three words never mean *'Can we talk?'*. They mean, *'Can I break up with you and still be friends?'*.

"Sure," I say, the words catching in my throat as I swallow hard. The beginning of an anxiety attack is looming, threatening to suffocate me with its intensity. This is why I keep people at arm's length to protect myself from pain and rejection. Yet, at this moment, it feels as though I'm completely exposed and in danger of the sting of rejection.

Xavier must sense my tension because he quickly tries to fill the awkward silence by saying, "Not *'that talk'*, Joy. Today is not the day your world comes collapsing down around you."

Oh, great, but you're saying there's a chance you'll hurt me in the future.

"The other day I told you I love you, you said nothing, and that's okay. Even before we had sex, I knew you were someone special that I could spend my time with. Maybe all my time. But you're making Harper an issue in our relationship. You are," he reiterates.

"Harper has done nothing to insert herself into our business. How can I help you through this?" he asks.

"You can't, and you're right. It's my issue to deal with, not yours. I need to decide not to let her bother me or to move on. That may sound harsh, but it's my reality, and it's up to me to decide. We are complete opposites."

"Are you, though? How can you even say that? You have no idea who she is."

"See, there you go, defending her again."

He laughs, but I can tell it's more from exhaustion over this conversation than genuine laughter. "Joy, I'm not defending Harper; I'm fighting for us."

Is this what he's been doing the whole time? Did I think he was defending her when he was clearly fighting to keep us together despite mine and Harper's differences?

Pushing all logic aside because I sabotage good things in my life, apparently, I add, "And she played a part in the break-up between Gabe and me."

"Did she though?" Xavier questions me again, but he's not looking for an answer and continues, "Because everything I watched transpire was: she got a job, and he couldn't leave her alone. He pursued her, Joy, not the other way around. You keep saying you're not mad about it, but you clearly are, and you're clearly not over Gabe because this comes up too often." His face falls, and his eyes grow a little darker as a raw vulnerability shines through him; he's clearly hurt by not only my words but my actions as well.

I argue, "This isn't about Gabe, the person. Gabe and I were still friends after we broke up and continued to hang out strictly platonic. But once he and Harper committed to each other, he never reached out again. Gabe is just another person who meant a lot to me and bailed on me for the next best thing." I look down at the ground, having a hard time making eye contact with Xavier.

"I understand, and thank you for finally being honest with me. Have you talked to Gabe about your feelings?" he asks.

"No, of course not. There's no reason to; he's with Harper. He made his choice. Honestly, Xavier, Gabe the person isn't worth it. My issue with Gabe choosing her over me is I feel like everyone in my life chooses someone or something over me."

After a few minutes of silence and what feels like could be the end of us, he asks, "Is there any way we can meet for coffee and talk, just the three of us? Without Gabe. Maybe it'll help you see who she is under her harsh exterior and allow her to appreciate who you are."

I play out a few scenarios in my head. In one of them, she is swinging me around by my ponytail. In the other scenario, I jump off the small table and land on top of her like something from a WWE wrestling match. Both scenarios make me laugh to myself. Roxy's words come to mind: *Maybe you can try with Harper?'* so I reluctantly agree to meet her and Xavier for a coffee.

Chapter 20

As I walk into the coffee shop, my stomach is in knots. I can't remember the last time I felt this nervous, and the worst part is it's over a girl. A girl that I've been actively avoiding for the past year or so in our apartment building. Pretending I'm reading something on my phone if we get in the elevator together, conducting fake phone calls if I have to walk by her in the lobby. All in the name of avoidance. I know, not some of my finest moments. I've never denied that my conflict resolution skills are much to be desired.

Maybe it's dread and not nerves at all. Yes, I'm going with dread. It's definitely dread I'm feeling.

Harper's already sat at a table in the corner when Xavier and I enter the coffee shop. She's wearing high-rise jeans that make her legs look two miles long even sitting down and a tight black bodysuit showing her perfect midsection. There are three coffees already on the table. *How did she know what to order me?* She sees us, smiles at Xavier, and waves at him. I'm not sure I've ever seen her smile; it's nice. We approach the table just as Harper stands to hug Xavier, looks at me, then proceeds to sit down. Off to a perfect start, I think to myself.

Harper says to me, "I'm glad you came today."

I'm so suspicious of her intentions that it's nearly impossible for me to think anything she says is genuine, and I have no idea why.

"Yeah, me too," I say cautiously.

There is no denying the awkwardness of the meeting. Any onlooker would be able to see how uncomfortable all of us are. Xavier is nervous, for good reason. I am skeptical of everything at this point, and Harper, well, Harper is Harper… impossible to read.

I pick up the coffee that is sitting there for me, and admit it's exactly what I would've ordered for myself.

"So you don't like me, and you don't want Xavier and I to talk anymore." She looks me dead in the eye before she says, "You do know we're family, right? Like bound by blood type of family."

Okay, so we're just going to cut straight to the point, no hellos, or how are you on this fine day?

I look at Xavier for help, but his face is buried in his latte cup, which is the size of a soup bowl.

I'm torn between jumping into self-preservation mode and running away or staying and being vulnerable. Do I tell her how I really feel or put up a wall to protect myself? Trying to muster up enough self-respect, I say, "I didn't ask Xavier not to talk to you. I said that you and I have zero in common and we'll never be friends. I also asked if you two weren't cousins, would you even like each other? I also said it makes me uncomfortable and I find it hard to trust you because of what happened after Gabe and I broke things off."

"What do you mean?" she asks, I think, genuinely confused.

"Gabe and I were good after he broke things off. He even came to me for advice about you. But once you two started seriously dating, he stopped all communication with me, which

I can only assume came from you."

Harper interrupts, "You know what they say about assuming, don't you?"

I shake my head.

She continues, "I never asked Gabe not to talk to you or ghost you. He and I have been together pretty much non-stop since my birthday. I think you're reading way too far into this. I know his feelings for you, and I know his feelings for me. From what I can see, Gabe was always honest with you, so why all the assumptions?"

Then, because she's Harper, she adds, "And as far as you and I being friends. I don't remember ever asking for such a relationship, but let me ask you, why do you say that we could never be friends?"

"I don't know, Harper, we're just too different."

She chuckles and says, "Joy, you don't even know me. You know what Xavier has told you; you know what your perception is of me, but you've never even given me an opportunity to show you who I am, and based on how this conversation is going, you never will." Her voice carries a hint of frustration, yet there's an honest edge to it.

And I think she's right. I'm not sure I'll allow myself to give her a chance to show me who she really is. And with that, I say, "If you two will excuse me, my phone is vibrating in my purse non-stop. It must be work. I have to grab it." I get up and walk outside to gather myself and get some air. I'm half tempted to leave and just text Xavier that I had an emergency at work and to meet me later, but I'm a sales manager at a car dealership. We don't have emergencies, and Harper, of all people, knows that. So, I stand outside, pretend I'm on the phone, and watch their interaction.

Harper says something casually to Xavier while she sits

back in her chair.

Xavier runs his fingers through his hair and then rests his elbows on the table with his head buried in his hands.

Harper leans in, takes his hand, and says something I can't make out.

Xavier gives Harper a side-eye look, and she deflates as she says something else to him.

Through my peripherals, I can see Harper about to get up to leave, so before I lose my courage, I walk inside to take this opportunity to make things right and finally put this behind us. Walking back to the table, I realize I'm no longer nervous. There are no butterflies or knots; I sit down and look directly at Harper.

"Listen, Harper, I owe you an apology. I owe Xavier an apology as well, but I'll deal with him later." My tone says more than my words will ever portray. For the first time, I think I see the Harper Xavier has been telling me about.

She puts her hand on mine and says, "I just want us to try to get to know each other." She pulls her hand away and plays nervously with her napkin as she continues, "I know when you and Gabe were together, you tried to be nice to me, and I never made any effort to reciprocate the gesture. Honestly, Joy, I don't know where you and I will end up. I know that Xavier is my family and best friend, and I love him dearly. Would we be friends if we weren't related? Deep down I think we would. He is the most amazing person I've ever met and not to mention how silly we are together. I don't want him to feel he has to choose because he'd choose you right now. Will he harbor animosity toward you later? Maybe, maybe not. Will it eventually come between you? Maybe, maybe not. But I want him to be happy, and you seem to make him happy."

She's not wrong. I may win in the short term but making

him choose between his family and someone he's known for a second will blow up in my face. He'll miss her because he genuinely loves her.

I ask, "Do you think it'll be uncomfortable for you and Gabe to be around me?"

She answers without hesitation, "Um, yes, defiantly. It'll be awkward as fuck." She laughs. "But we'll ease into it. Xavier and Gabe don't spend a lot of time together. Most of the time, it's just Xavier and I meeting like this for coffee, but I don't want you to feel uncomfortable around me because of Gabe. I completely understand where you're coming from and can't say that I would feel any different than you, but I don't want you to feel uncomfortable because that's not fair to you."

She takes a deep breath then adds, "I know I'm babbling at this point. What I'm trying to say is I get it, and I'm sorry. I transferred stores to try to make things right by you two, but six months later, he was in my apartment waiting for me. It was hard to say no again." She shrugs as she finishes her explanation, and I understand. She pushed him away for months because of me and then couldn't anymore.

I don't say anything immediately while trying to digest her confession's gravity. And for the second time today, I truly believe her. I know what she said is genuine, and it's not just to make Xavier happy.

"Okay," I say.

"Okay?" she repeats but in a question.

"I think we can make something work, or at least we owe it to Xavier and ourselves to try. Honestly, Harper, I'm so sorry for trying to drive a wedge between you and Xavier. I'm sorry he didn't feel like he could be honest with you about us—"

"That's on him, not on you, Joy," Harper interrupts, and I nod in agreement.

Harper adds, "Joy, can I tell you something else?"

I look at her and nod.

She says, "Xavier is the only person in the world who knows everything about me. I have never trusted anyone with my secrets as I trust him. He makes it so easy to be honest and open with."

I feel everything she is saying with all my soul because he's only the second person I've shared my childhood secrets and fears with. But there's a strange pit in my stomach that feels like jealousy. Xavier is that person not only for me but for her as well. And, it's at this point I realize I'll always have to share some part of him with Harper.

Chapter 21

My phone rings, and it's Harper. A few months have passed since our come-to-Jesus moment at the coffee shop. Are we best friends? Absolutely not. Are we enemies? Nope, not that either. As much as it pains me to say it, Harper Atwood isn't as terrible as I made her out to be, and I don't mind spending time with her. Is it weird to listen to her plan her wedding to my ex-boyfriend? At first, it was, but now I don't even see him as an ex. My life with Xavier is much more fulfilling than with Gabe. The conversations are deeper and more meaningful. The sex is next level. What I had with Gabe was superficial and forced. Although I'm thankful for the relationship I had with Gabe, I'm home when I'm with Xavier.

My phone vibrates, and Roxanne shows up on my screen. I quickly answer and hit the speaker button.

"Have you tried to back out of going to the wedding today?" she asks.

"What do you mean, have I tried to back out? Of course not. I'm going!"

"He's your ex, and just a few months ago, she was your sworn enemy!" she yells into the phone.

"And you told me I needed to grow up, so I did," I yell back at her.

"And that's it?" she asks. "Since when do you listen to me?"

We chuckle and I say, "I don't know, Roxy; I guess I don't care enough about whatever Gabe and I were not to forgive her. Maybe I don't have any more room for grudges?"

"Just so long as you're comfortable and don't feel forced."

"I know you're looking out for me, but I haven't been with Gabe in over a year, and I've been with Xavier for longer than I was ever with Gabe. He means way more to me than Gabe ever did. And, as far as Harper—" I pause to think of how to describe our friendship without having Roxy feeling like she needs to protect me. "We're more than acquaintances but not quite friends. I don't know, Roxy. You're the one who kept suggesting that maybe it was me and not her all along. Well, I'm not too proud to admit it was mostly me, with a little bit of her sprinkled in. Like sixty/forty." I chuckle. "You said I needed to accept her for Xavier's sake. And I've taken your advice. Have you ever had to do something you didn't want to do with Christopher?" I ask.

"All the time," she answers way too voluntarily.

"Okay, well, think of today as one of those things for me. I could stay home while Xavier watches his best friend get married off, or I could be there with him." I add, "I don't know, Roxy; I'm just winging it now. Think of the bright side. After tonight, Harper will be married and unable to steal another of my men."

We both laugh, and she asks, "Should I say have fun?"

"Well, that's better than saying have a shitty time," I say with a smile.

"You know what I mean," she says annoyed.

"I have to go," I say. "I have to outshine the bride."

And then we laugh again.

A knock on my door reminds me how late I'm running.

"Come in. It's open," I yell from my bathroom.

"Not safe," Xavier says as he lets himself in.

"I know," I yell back down the hall to him.

He walks back toward the bathroom wearing a black tux, and I freeze. Xavier always looks good in dress and casual clothes, but tonight, he's perfection. He's wearing slim-fit tuxedo pants, a white shirt, a black vest, and a tie with a black jacket. His blue eyes are the only hint of color on his body and are mesmerizing.

"Poor Gabe. No one will be looking in his direction tonight," I say.

Xavier gives me a sweet smile, but there's a warning in it as well. A promise of what's to come later, and there's a rush of heat that courses through me, igniting anticipation between my legs.

"Are you almost ready?" he asks, tapping his foot at me with his arms crossed.

He's in the wedding party. Since Harper has only one other friend, Xavier will stand beside her.

"Yes, I just need you to zip me up." I remove my robe and have nothing under it.

Xavier looks at my naked body and shakes his head.

"You're going to do this to me right now?" he asks.

"No, I can't wear undergarments with this dress because they show."

He looks at me with an intrigued smile. I grab my dress off the hanger, which slides down my body, waterfalling like when the opera's curtain closes at the show's end. My long black sheath dress is tight with a low back and a v in the front.

"Damn," Xavier says, "you look sublime."

"Sublime?" I question.

"Beautiful, gorgeous, breathtaking. Pick one. We don't have time for this today," he jokes.

"Oh okay, well thank you, good sir," I reply. "Now, would you be so kind as to zip me up?"

"Only if I can unzip you later," he says as he takes the small delicate zipper in his hand and slowly pulls it up by the back. Looking like he wants to devour me the entire time.

"I'd be disappointed if you didn't." I wink at him, grab his hand, and we go.

Chapter 22

I'll never complain about waking up to the sun shining through Xavier's open window. The man has no blinds, shades, or curtains in his apartment—not one. He hates to block natural light; I, on the other hand, have blackout curtains on every window.

Since we've been together, I leave mine open more often and enjoy the natural sunlight.

Xavier has changed me. He's made me a little less scared and a lot more vulnerable; if he left me tomorrow, I'd be okay, though, and I don't think that's normal. Is it a protective mechanism in my brain since everyone in my past has left me, or am I just broken? I'm not sure either one of those is a better alternative over the other, but dwelling on things like this puts me back into a shitty childhood state of mind that I'd prefer not to get lost in.

"Good morning," Xavier says in a raspy, hungover voice.

"Good morning," I say in an 'I told you not to drink so much' voice.

"Can we just stay here all day?" Xavier begs.

"You can, but I can't. I promised Roxy I would meet her for lunch today and fill her in on last night's festivities."

With an eye roll, he says, "I'll never understand girls."

"We were not made to be understood," I say unapologetically.

After a shower and a fresh face, an hour later, I'm rushing out of the door to meet Roxy. After a night of champagne-filled toasts, there will be no day drinking for this girl today. I head down to the parking garage to grab my car. Xavier was back asleep when I left, and I didn't want to wake him, so I text him with a winky emoji to let him know I'll be home around two pm. Then I send a short text to Rox, letting her know I'm heading her way.

My favorite song is on the radio, and it has me feeling good about how special Xavier made me feel last night. He wanted to make sure I wasn't uncomfortable. He introduced me to his mom and Harper's family. He barely left my side all night; when he did, his mom was there to take his place. Harper looked beautiful in her dress. It was white with a lace bodice, then at the waist, it flared out like a bell, and it was all tulle. Layers and layers of tulle. Where Roxanne looked like she walked out of a fairy tale, Harper looked like she walked out of a bridal magazine.

A horn beeps behind me to alert me that the light is green and pulls me from my thoughts. I look in my rear and wave a sorry. I exit the intersection, and before I can react, a car is speeding right toward my driver's door. Filled with pure terror, I instinctively try to hit the gas pedal to speed up and avoid the crash, but it's not enough to escape the car speeding right at me, oblivious to the red light he's about to run. My car is the only thing between him and several people in the crosswalk. I look through my passenger window to see at least ten people laughing and carrying on as they casually cross the street. Then I look back to the speeding car, and it's that exact moment I know I won't be making it to lunch today.

My cell phone flies out of my cup holder with the force of a bullet and shatters as it hits the passenger window. There is no screeching of tires. Only screams of strangers fill the air. My radio still plays my favorite song, helping to drown out the panic outside my car. I don't try to move; I stay there slumped over, lying on my center console, listening to my favorite song. I try to open my eyes, but when I do, a warm liquid running from my head fills them. I squeeze my eyelids shut, trying to stop the burning. As shock takes over my body, I become numb to the pain, and exhaustion takes over, filling me with an overwhelming need to sleep. I still don't attempt to move because the desire for rest is much more significant than the need to move. In the distance, I can hear sirens approaching. It's a mix of sounds coming from different emergency vehicles. One is loud and short, while one is more profound with a long whaling sound. Quickly, the sirens drown out the onlookers' screams. People have surrounded my car with a barrage of questions.

"Ma'am, can you move?"

"Miss, are you okay?"

I can't see how many people are out there, but several voices echo in the small cab of my car. I can't answer them. No words will leave my mouth that's filled with metallic liquid. Did the impact make me bite my tongue, because the taste of copper is heavy in my mouth.

I hear a man's voice closer and calmer than the others; "Don't fall asleep; the ambulance is on its way. Hold on and fight for a few more minutes. Don't try to move; the paramedics will get you out. Hang in there. Don't panic. You're going to be okay."

Chapter 23

The beeping won't stop—*beep, beep, beep*. I moan and try to say hello, but my mouth feels like I ate four pounds of sand. I clear my throat as best I can and whisper, "Hello."

A nurse rushes in and says lovingly, "Well, hello, sleepy head." She doesn't sound much older than I am, maybe a year or two older.

"Can I get some water?" is what I try to ask, but I know it sounds nothing like I intended.

She understands me, though, because a second later I hear her pour water into a cup. She puts a straw in my mouth, and I instinctively suck the straw. Pain radiates through my body, and I wince. I feel every organ wake up as the water runs down my esophagus. I squeeze my eyes closed in agony, and she says, "Yeah, I know, you're going to hurt for a bit. You got hit pretty hard. I will get the doctor on call to talk to you. Do you feel up to it?"

Do I feel up to it? I just woke up; I feel like I got hit by a train, and I'm alone. I look at my nurse and slowly shake my head no.

My nurse says, "Your very handsome boyfriend just left about an hour ago to shower and change. He'll be back anytime now. And your best friends, Roxanne and Harper, should also be back soon."

Harper, what the hell? Why has she been here?

"How long have I been here?" I'm finally able to get out a coherent question.

"Two weeks," she says as she rubs my hand.

I open my eyes wide, and she gives me a pitying smile, clearly seeing the confusion and surprise in my expression.

"You saved many lives by pulling in front of that car."

In silence, I shake my head no in confusion.

She continues, "The car that hit you was intentionally trying to run down everyone in the crosswalk, but when you pulled out and stopped in the intersection, you stopped him. There was a note in his car detailing all his intentions. You're a hero, Joy."

"I didn't do that," I whisper.

"Tell that to the twenty-five witnesses that say you, in fact, did do that."

I want to argue and explain what happened, but it hurts. Everything hurts so bad.

She continues, "Joy, there were no other cars around you; it was just you and him. The videos show you look and see him coming. You looked at the pedestrians, pulled to the middle of the intersection, and prepared yourself for impact. When the closed caption footage from the streetlights was released, it went viral, and then, of course, all the onlookers released their cell phone video as well. We've had reporters and journalists bombarding your room for two weeks. Your boyfriend has been keeping them at bay."

"Can you wake me when Xavier gets here, please?"

"No need; he's walking in now," she says with excitement in her voice. "She's awake. I'll give you guys a few minutes to yourself, but not too long. I need to tell the doctor you're awake."

Xavier fidgets slightly, his hands moving restlessly. His eyes wander around the room, avoiding direct eye contact. I can tell he doesn't know how to act, so I try to ease the tension.

"Sorry, I wasn't home at two pm like I promised."

"How do you feel? Are you okay?" he asks. "Fuck, Joy, I've been worried sick," he says he approaches my bed and rubs his hands over his face. By the dark circles under his eyes, he hasn't been sleeping or eating.

"I feel like I got hit by a car," I answer him.

He nods. "Babe I've been dying inside. I've been so worried about you."

He sits next to me on my bed, and my insecurities take over, and a panic attack threatens as my heart races. He looks up at the monitor and then back at me.

"Are you okay?" he asks with a bit of trepidation in his voice. *Fucking machine, allow me no secrets.* I nod my head, yes.

"If you need to go—" is all I manage to get out before he interrupts me.

"What?" he sounds offended. "I've been here twenty-two hours a day talking to your unconscious body, pleading with you to wake up. Do you know how scared I've been that I would lose you and I wouldn't be able to spend the rest of my life with my soulmate? Now that you're finally awake, you want me to leave?" he asks as he shoves the palms of his hands in his eyes.

Soulmate? Live without me? I haven't even told him I love him, and he's calling me his soulmate. Am I dreaming?

I try to reach out and touch him, only to realize I can't move anything on my body.

"Xavier, I can't move anything on my body, can I?" Panic

builds in my voice.

He looks down at his feet. "No, not yet," he mumbles.

I say nothing as tears fill my eyes. There's no way he's going to stick around for the amount of physical therapy needed to get me to walk again, if that's even possible. The heart monitor starts to beep faster and faster again.

"Stop, Joy. Don't let your wonderful head wander off to dark places. I'm not going anywhere."

Just then, Roxanne and Harper walk in. The moment I see Roxy, the tears that have been welling up in my eyes for the past thirty seconds spill over, rushing down my face like a waterfall.

Holding back her tears, Roxanne cries, "Stop it right now. I can't cry today; I've cried every day for two weeks. Stop this shit right now."

"I can't move, let alone walk, Roxanne; what will I do?" I say through my tears. The reality of not having a grandma, a loving dad, or a typical mom hits me harder than it has in a long time.

I continue to cry and say, "I live alone, Roxanne. I live on the third floor of my apartment building. How did this happen? How am I going to take care of myself?"

"Well, you obviously didn't want to meet me for lunch, so you parked your car in the middle of the intersection to save a bunch of pedestrians and ended up here. Maybe next time you say, '*Hey Rox, not in the mood, I'll see you at work Monday.*'"

I laugh a little and then wince at the pain that reverberates through my entire body.

Then Harper chimes in, "What do you mean you're alone? Girl, we've been here for the past two weeks, sleeping on couches, hospital beds, and dirty floors. If that doesn't make us family, I don't know what does."

Roxanne looks at Xavier, silently encouraging him to speak. He takes a deep breath and says, "As for living alone and taking care of yourself. I was thinking you could move into my apartment since I live on the first floor. I've already talked to my work and cleared it with them so I can take time off and work remotely until you are back on your feet. I'll be available to take you to all your doctor appointments. I'm going to take care of you from now on."

"Xavier, you didn't have to do that," I say.

"I know I didn't; I wanted to. I want to take care of you and be there for you. You're not alone, Joy. You have not only Roxanne but me as well."

"And me!" Harper chimes in again.

Xavier continues, "We'll get through this together."

Just then, a doctor in his mid-fifties with light hair and medium build walks in. "Well, well, our hero is finally awake from her nap," he says.

I smile at him.

"You ready for the details and next steps?" He's a little too chipper to share the news that I may never walk again. He reaches into his crisp white coat, pulls out a light pen, and shines it into my eyes.

I squint.

"Good," he says. "Perfect."

Roxy is doing the happy dance behind him as if I just scored a touchdown.

"Here's where we are, Joy. You had extensive internal injuries besides the external ones. You've been here for two weeks, which allowed many of your cuts and bruises to heal. You have two shattered femurs, a broken shoulder…"

"Is that all?" I interrupt like it's just another day at the office.

"I know it's a lot," he says as he pats my hand. "The

concussion is better now. The CT scans of your brain are perfect. Our pressing issues are: how do we get you walking with two broken legs? We don't is the answer," he says. "Your broken back is what is stopping you from moving your limbs. But we can't start physical therapy until your legs can bear your weight and your shoulder is healed. So, for a bit, we're in a holding period."

"So, what do I do?" I ask, stressed out of mind but doing what I think is a pretty a good job holding it together.

"You'll hang out here with us. This will allow your nurses to make sure you don't get bed sores on your backside, keep you clean, and manage your pain. We'll do a little physical therapy here in your room a few times a day to make sure you don't lose all your muscles. This is to remind your body that it once worked without forcing it.

"Um, okay," I agree because what else am I supposed to say?

Chapter 24

"Are you ready?" Roxanne asks in an overly excited voice.

"You have no idea." I've been in the hospital for three months. My legs and shoulders are healed. I've lost eighteen pounds that I didn't think I had to lose, but my doctors say a lot of it is lost muscle, and it'll be easy to put back on once I start eating real food again. The food here is terrible. If there's anyone who got the short end of the stick, it's Xavier, because he's been here every day since the accident just like he said he would be. He works from the cafeteria on the days I have longer physical therapy sessions. My arms are working now that the swelling in my spine is down. My several back surgeries were successful. Now, it's just a matter of getting my legs to move. I can lift myself into a wheelchair, which is why they're finally letting me leave.

I agreed to move in with Xavier, so he's been spending a few hours away from the hospital setting up *our* new apartment.

"The apartment is all set up and ready for you," Xavier says as he helps me sit up and swing my legs so they're dangling from my bed. He then lifts me like a baby and sets me in my chair. I look up at him, and tears fill my eyes. I want to feel sorry for myself, but I can't because my guilt for putting him through this is my overriding emotion.

"Don't do it, Joy," he says. Do not start crying because you feel like a burden or that you're disappointing me. I don't want to go round and round with you about this."

I nod in concession.

"Are you ready to blow this popsicle stand?" Roxanne says.

I shake my head and say, "Sometimes, I feel like you're a sixty-year-old woman trapped in a twenty-year-old body."

She puts her hands on her hips and wiggles them at me.

Xavier puts me in his car, and all the flashbacks of that day come racing back. My chest clinches, and tears roll down my face. Xavier gets in his side of the car and looks at me. All I see in his eyes is empathy.

I look at him and reassure him, "I'm okay. I promise. It's just a lot to digest right now. I've been hidden in a hospital room for months, barely getting any sunlight. So, being outside is overwhelming without riding in a car right away."

"I get it," Xavier says in an understanding voice.

He buckles my seatbelt, and we drive overly slow home, so slow it's hard for me not to laugh.

"I'm driving slow, so the bumps don't hurt you," he explains.

"Yes, the bumps that I can't feel because I'm paralyzed don't hurt me; that is why you're driving slow," I joke.

As we pull up to the front of his apartment, Roxanne is waiting to take me up while Xavier parks his car. He pulls into the loading area, gets my wheelchair from the back, picks me out of the car, and sets me in my chair. He looks at Roxy. They give each other a fist bump as if they're in a relay race, and I'm the handoff.

"Good thing you guys like each other," I say.

"I love him," Roxy reassures me as she pulls me through

the front door of his apartment backward. When she turns me around, I scan the room, and it's a perfect combination of Xavier's and my furniture and décor. There's a handrail in the bathroom near the toilet, and the shower is wheelchair accessible with a shower chair ready for my first shower at home.

I look at Roxanne and ask, "How will this work? I feel like Xavier and I skipped dating to him changing my diapers and showering me. How did this happen?" I say, shaking my head.

"It's fine, Joy. Stop overthinking this," Roxanne demands.

"Can you help me out of this to the couch?" I ask her.

"No, I can't, Joy; we have to wait for Xavier."

"Why? I'll do most of the work, I promise. I need you to make sure I don't fall," I retort, growing frustrated.

Roxanne lowers herself to her knees so we're face to face, and she says, "You're going to be auntie; I can't lift you." She pauses and adds, "I'm sorry it's not a good time; it just happened."

"What!" I squeal. "Tell me everything! Is it a girl or a boy, and when are you due? How long have you been keeping this from me?"

Xavier walks in and says, "I heard her from down the hall. I'm assuming that means you finally told her."

"*What!* You told his guy before me?" I shriek as I point at Xavier.

Using her hands to calm me down, Roxy says, "Whoa, whoa. I had to tell him for logistic purposes."

I roll my eyes, knowing she's not wrong. "*Well!*" I exclaim.

Roxy screams, "She's a girl!"

I scream, and Xavier shakes his head, and he lifts me from my chair and places me on the couch.

She continues as if Xavier isn't even there. "I'm nineteen weeks, so I'll start showing any day now." She goes over to her bag, pulls a book from her purse, and hands it to me. *All the Things a First-Time Auntie Needs to Know* is the title, and of course, I cry again, but this time, my tears trigger her tears, and Xavier makes a dash for the bedroom and stays there to give us space.

Chapter 25

"What's the occasion?" I ask as Xavier helps me into a black dress that hasn't fit since the accident.

"No occasion he answers, just dinner with Roxy, Christopher, Harper, and Gabe."

"Fuck," I exclaim.

"You forgot?" he asks, but it's not a question because he knows the answer already. I've been very forgetful since the accident, which is expected according to all my doctors. They say it's a combination of my concussion as well as the trauma.

"I'm sorry," I say.

"Don't apologize, Joy. Do you want me to call them and cancel?" He's sincere and not a sign of frustration.

"No, no, it's fine, I'm good. I'm sorry, I just—" I stop talking because I'm not sure how many times I apologize to this man for forgetting shit.

The doorbell rings, and Xavier yells from the bedroom, "On my way!"

He lifts me from the bed into my chair, and off we go to the front door. Xavier ordered takeout, and Harper picked it up and brought it with her. She and Roxy set the table and get everything ready. I help by getting beers for the guys. Since Roxy is pregnant and I'm taking a million different prescriptions, we're sticking with water tonight.

Dinner is quiet at first. The atmosphere feels heavy, like when you wake up at the beach on a cold California morning. The air is heavy, and the sand is thick and wet. All eyes are on me, and I can't take the silence anymore.

I blurt out, "Okay, you're all allowed two questions, and then we're talking about something else."

Everyone chuckles, which eases some of the tension. I haven't seen Gabe since their wedding, and I've only seen Christopher once for a few minutes at the hospital. Something is bothering Gabe; he's never had a good poker face, and tonight is no different. There's something he wants to ask or say but doesn't.

Christopher asks, "Why did you do it, Joy?"

Everyone's heads snap in his direction just as Roxy slaps him in the arm.

If anyone was going to ask an honest question, I knew it would be him. Roxy and Xavier asked me the question before, but it was in jest, and they never expected an answer from me. The two of them have been walking on eggshells since I woke up from my coma months ago. No thoughtful questions, no re-living the accident. There is no real talk about feelings. Maybe they're afraid I'll have a breakdown, and neither of them are equipped emotionally to deal with that. So, it's all casual conversation and medically necessary questions.

I take a deep breath then answer Christopher as honestly as possible, "I think there are two answers to this question." My voice trembles slightly as I set my fork down.

"One answer is, on a conscious level, I don't think I can articulate a response that anyone other than myself would truly understand. But subconsciously, I think I did what I did because I've never felt sincerely protected. Growing up, your parents are supposed to love and protect you unconditionally, but I wasn't afforded that luxury. Instead, I had my grandparents who, by circumstance, left me here alone." My voice softens as memories of the accident flood my mind.

"I saw several people, some mere children, who had no idea that tragedy was about to rain down on them. I saw mothers who didn't have time to shield their children; I saw children with years left to live and husbands who wouldn't have otherwise made it home to their families." Tears sting the backs of my eyes, and Xavier puts his hand on mine to comfort me. I look between Roxanne and Xavier.

"As much I love you both, despite what Harper said that day in the hospital, you guys are technically not my family. So, I could keep families together by putting myself between that car and those people in the crosswalk. I was able to save fathers so they could protect their kids and save mothers from losing their children because they didn't have enough time to react to tragedy." My voice trembles with emotion.

Harper and Roxanne are crying now.

"Xavier, you would've missed me; I know this with every fiber of my being, but you still have Harper and your mom. Roxy, you have Christopher and your family. In the grand scheme of things, my life is insignificant and just a tiny pawn in a much larger plan."

Everyone is silent and not moving. At this point, I can't even say for sure if they're breathing.

Christopher asks, "You mentioned a honk that came from behind you. There is no evidence of that. You were alone."

I reply, "I don't know, Christopher; in my mind, I heard a horn honk behind me as if to alert me to go. I looked in my rear-view mirror and waved at the car behind me to thank him, and I pulled out."

Christopher says again, "But you know that didn't happen?"

Roxanne hits him again.

"No, Roxanne, it's okay." I continue, "I understand from all the videos I've seen that it didn't happen. Why I have a memory of that, I can't explain. but I can honestly say I didn't do it to be a hero." I've avoided reporters, journalists, bloggers, and almost-victims. I don't want recognition; I don't want praise. I want to forget it ever happened, which is impossible because this fucking chair is a daily reminder.

Harper clears her throat and quietly asks, "Do you believe in angels?"

"I don't know," I answer honestly. "What relevance does that have on this, though?"

She rubs her thighs, clearly nervous about what she's about to say. "Can we all agree that with the force of that impact, you should be dead?"

Xavier gives her a look at death, and Gabe does as well.

Typical Harper, not noticing them or caring, continues, "What I mean is, no one died. You didn't die, nor did any of the pedestrians in the crosswalk."

Surprised by this side of Harper, I ask, "But why all that to leave me here in a wheelchair?"

"That's a question we'll never have an answer to because, hopefully, you'll be out of it soon," she says in the most genuine, loving voice I've ever heard from her.

"I don't know," I say. "I don't feel like a hero; I never tried to be a hero. In my mind, this was all an accident. An unfortunate one that's left me unable to walk."

"For now," Xavier interjects.

Chapter 26

Xavier dries my hair from the edge of our bed. "What's on your mind?" he asks.

"Nothing," I answer.

He looks at me with one raised eyebrow, a tell that he doesn't believe me.

"I feel bad; I know this is not how you saw us when you first asked me on a date."

"No, when I first asked you on a date, Joy, I just wanted to get to know this smoking-hot woman who had literally bumped into my world, knocking everything off course. And then after that, I envisioned us growing old together and getting through life's challenges without either feeling guilty about taking care of the other one," he softly speaks.

"Listen, Joy, I know Roxanne is your rock, and you feel you can share anything and everything with her. I hope I can also be that person for you someday."

More guilt runs through my body because here I am, literally dependent on this man, feeling guilty about it, and he's asking for more of me.

"Xavier, I love you. Thank you for caring for me."

He smiles and says, "Baby, you've never said I love you. I

love you too, Joy."

Although Xavier told me he loved me before the accident, he doesn't have to say it. Everything he's done for me the last several months shows me he does, which means more than any three words. He lifts me out of my chair and sets me on the side of the bed like he always does to help me dress and undress.

He helps me out of my dress and tries to walk over to my dresser for my pajamas, but before he can get too far, I grab him by the wrist and pull him back to me. He kneels in front of me to see what's wrong.

"Kiss me?" I ask in a whisper.

He does, and I'm overcome with passion flowing through my veins. It's been so long since we shared a kiss like this that I lose myself in him. I feel alive after so many months of feeling numb.

"Will you have sex with me?" I ask.

"Joy, I don't want to hurt you," he says.

"I got hit by a car, Xavier. As good as you are in bed, I don't think you can hurt me any worse than I've been hurt."

Under a chuckle, he says, "You know what I mean."

"Let's just try. If it's too much; we'll stop. I need this. I need intimacy; I need to show you how much I love and appreciate you; I need you inside me."

"I love you forever Joy." He says as he kisses the top of my head.

I unzip his pants the best I can, and he stands to allow them to fall to the floor. He removes his boxers, and it's clear he needs this as much as I do. I put the tip of him inside my mouth, and I suck the pre-cum that is already dripping. I take his hips and pull his entire length inside my mouth, which forces a moan from his lips.

He wraps my hair around his fists. "Baby, it's been so long; I've missed fucking you so much."

I continue to pull him by his hips in and out of my mouth until he pulls out of my mouth and he lowers himself onto me. He gently places each of his open palms on my knees and spreads my legs. He slowly takes his cock and guides it between my folds and then slowly, gently, he enters me. He lowers his head, moaning again, and rests it on my breasts. This interaction is like nothing I've ever experienced. He is gentle, and loving. He slowly pulls in and out of me, and within minutes, I feel my orgasm cresting.

"Xavier, I'm going to orgasm."

"I am, too. I'll be careful."

I put my hands on both of his hips and pull him into me as deep as our bodies will allow. I feel him tremble in my arms as he's about to orgasm. His body tenses as he tries to fight the urge to power into me. Slowly, he continues to slide in and out of me. He reaches down between my legs and rubs my clit. Instantly, my orgasm hits me like a wave of pleasure.

"It's okay. You're not going to hurt me."

He lets out a final moan as his orgasm rolls over him, allowing us to orgasm together.

Breathless, he whispers in my ear, "Marry me, Joy."

Chapter 27

We lay in bed, the moon lighting up the room just enough for me to see Xavier's eyes on me. Xavier installed blinds on all his windows before I moved in, but they were left open tonight, and I know Xavier is too tired to get up to close them.

"What's on your mind?" I ask, looking at the reflection of the moon bounce off our ceiling.

"You didn't answer my question," he says in an almost whisper.

I turn my head in his direction. "You were serious?"

He turns on his side and rests his head on his hand. "Of course I was serious. I know I don't have a ring, and it wasn't the most romantic setting, but I was on my knees." He chuckles.

"I just assumed you were lost in the moment."

"We'll go tomorrow and pick out rings if you tell me yes tonight," he insists.

"Xavier, you're on leave to take care of me. I'm on disability. The last thing you can afford is a ring."

He sits up entirely in bed and looks over to me. "Joy, don't make me ask you this a third time. Will you make me the happiest man in the world and share the rest of your life with me?"

"But I can't…"

He interrupts me, "Stop! Please don't say it. Don't you fucking say it, Joy. It's a yes or no question," he says.

I stare at him for a minute, deep into his sky-blue eyes. The darkness of our room shadows them, but they're there. He's here and will be here for me no matter what life throws at us. He's never going to leave me, wheelchair or not. He's stayed and has loved me unconditionally; besides my grandparents and Roxy, no one else ever has.

No matter how hard I tried to push him away and no matter how many chances I gave him to leave, he never did.

"Yes," I whisper. "Yes, I'll marry you, but I want to walk down the aisle."

"We'll start PT tomorrow."

And I know he means it.

Chapter 28

Physical therapy is an actual test of a person's mental and physical strength. There are times I want to cry, there are times I want to fight, but I'm consistently fighting the urge to give up. My PT isn't an hour of exercise and a nice massage and ice at the end. No, my PT is hours and hours of grueling pain. It's push-ups, pull-ups, and me balancing myself between two bars. It's Xavier helping me put one foot before the other as I hold all my body weight between those two bars. It's sit-ups and stretching, and it's every day because as much as I want to give up, I won't because I will walk down the aisle on the day of my wedding.

"Let's go, Joy, you got this. Keep pushing," Michael continues hollering at me.

I have never heard my name yelled more than when I'm here, and I played soccer my entire childhood! No coach has ever yelled my name more than Michael does.

Michael is my physical therapist and has been for the last few months. He's a bit older than me, maybe three years. He's tall and muscular, but I assume that's a prerequisite for the job. Has to be able to hold up dead weight for an ungodly period of time without collapsing.

"I'm trying… I'm trying," I cry out in pain. Sweat is dripping down my burning-hot face as I struggle to bear weight on my legs, all while holding myself up with just two scrawny toothpicks I call my arms. The room feels like it's a million degrees, and it makes me wonder why anyone would voluntarily walk into a hot yoga studio.

"I'm moving," I yell back at him.

"You're using too much arm; use more leg," Michael shouts as if we are worlds away from each other. He's standing ten feet away, but we continue to yell back and forth.

I try to will my body to use more leg, but nothing. Frustrated, I yell back, "You know I'm paralyzed, right, and my legs don't work, right?"

"They won't with that shitty attitude. Let's fight, Joy," Michael yells at me again.

So, I do; I continue to fight day after day so I can walk down the aisle on my wedding day.

Two hours later, fifty pounds of sweat lighter, Xavier picks me up and gingerly sets my exhausted body in my wheelchair.

"You did great," he says.

He's my biggest cheerleader, and I think I would've given up months ago if it hadn't been for him encouraging me. He says he could care less if I ever walk again, that he's perfectly fine carrying me from point A to point B, but he knows how important it is to me to walk again, so we continue to work, day after day.

"You hungry?" he asks, nodding his head up and down as if subconsciously willing me to say yes.

"I deserve pizza, don't you think?"

His smile is all I need to know I picked correctly.

Chapter 29

The alarm clock beeps, but I'm already awake. I didn't sleep at all last night. I tossed and turned and let my mind control me as I watched Xavier through all the different stages sleep has to offer.

He rolls over and asks, "Are you ready for today?"

"Yes, if you could help me up, I'll just brush my hair and teeth and be ready."

I have another surgery today for my spine. This is the last surgery I've agreed to have, and I don't think I would've agreed to it if I didn't want to walk down the aisle so badly when we get married. The surgeries are taking a toll on the half of my body that still works, as well as my hair and skin. I feel much older than I am, and each time, recovery is more complex and more challenging.

"You're quiet," Xavier says once we are in the car and driving.

"Yeah, sorry, a lot is riding on today."

"Yes, I know, and I'm confident today is the day, just promise me you won't keep pushing back the wedding."

"I promise," I lie. I've pushed back our wedding twice now. It was supposed to be six months ago, then three months ago, and now six months out. I'm not getting married in a wheelchair. Not because some asshole drove through an intersection and t-boned me.

After checking in downstairs, we take the elevator to the third floor, where the surgery waiting room is. I tell Xavier, "If I never see this hospital again, it'll be a blessing."

"I know," he says with a deep sigh. "Last one, babe, we got this."

"Yeah, last one," I say as my mind wanders to the big mean world of what-ifs.

The elevator doors open on the third floor, and any stranger would think I was having a birthday party today not surgery. Roxy, Christopher, and a very pregnant Harper and Gabe are here.

"What the hell are you all doing here?" I ask.

"Last one," Roxy says, holding a giant balloon and a big bouquet. "Besides, you'll be asleep soon, so we're here for Xavier."

I shake my head as she looks at me smugly as if to say, "Try to make me leave."

"Who has the baby?" I ask.

"My mom." She shakes her head. "Seriously, you're going in for surgery, and all you ask is who has my baby?" Roxanne and Christopher just had their baby girl Kadin three weeks ago, so, me asking about her isn't as crazy as she's making it out to be.

Harper holds a box of donuts, bagels, and enough coffee to fuel the surgical floor.

"For me?" I ask, reaching out my hands.

She glances at Xavier panicked, knowing damn, well, I can't have anything before surgery.

I smile and say, "If one of you M'fers opens that donut

box before I go into surgery, I'll run your feet over with my wheelchair!"

That earns me a laugh from Rox and a relieved sigh from Harper.

Looking at all my friends, I have an overwhelming feeling life is passing me by, and it is happening quickly. Roxanne has had Kadin, and Harper announced her pregnancy a month or so after I got out of the hospital. Roxanne's and Harper's kids will be just a few months apart, but that was supposed to be Roxy and me. That was our dream. I've pushed my wedding back twice and am about to do it for a third time. I will *walk* down that aisle. So, here I am at the hospital for yet another surgery, which will set me back another month or two.

The nurse quickly calls me back. I kiss Xavier and tell him I love him.

Roxy runs over before I go back and wraps her arms around my neck, kisses my forehead, and whispers, "I love you, Joy."

"I love you too, Rox. Oh, and today is not the day I'm dying, so relax. I'll see you in a few hours."

<h1 style="text-align:center">Chapter 30</h1>

I'm groggy and can't seem to wake up. I can hear Xavier trying to talk to me and rouse me to wake up, but my eyes are just too heavy. I listen to nurses coming and going and the familiar annoying sound of the blood pressure machine. *Beep… beep… beep.* That alone makes me want to stay asleep. Xavier shakes me a bit, and I open and close my eyes. He calls the nurse, and I hear him ask her if this is expected and that I can't wake up. She tries to reassure him that I am fine, but I hear the worry in his voice. I grab his hand and squeeze it to let him know I'm okay.

"You awake?" he asks.

I nod.

"Open your eyes, and look at me," he insists just as my doctor walks in.

"Xavier, she's fine, she's tired. We did a lot today, and she'll be in excruciating pain for the next week or so. She'll be tired for the next two days, but she is fine. Surgery was extensive. We're keeping her here for a few days. We're going to force physical therapy almost immediately. With the incisions, stitches, and trauma to her back, it'll be too much for you to manage getting her in and out of the chair alone. We're putting her in a large private room so you can stay and help us in physical therapy, so you'll be ahead of the game once I discharge her. Xavier, we got her legs to move, and we aren't willing to lose any progress."

• • •

I fight to awaken my senses and slowly pry my eyes open. It's quiet; no more beeping, just some faint sounds of nurses scurrying outside my room.

"Hey," I manage to croak out. My throat feels like I fell face-first into the sand at Santa Monica beach with my mouth open.

Xavier is on a couch on the other side of my room. He jumps up and hurries to my side.

"It's about damn time. Everyone is worried because you've been asleep for a full day."

"Tell them I'm alive. At least, I think I am. Maybe you should pinch me."

"Stop," Xavier says.

"What's the update?" I ask, and damn, does my throat hurt.

"They were able to have you move your legs in surgery, so now that you're awake, you can start PT."

"Oh, hell no, I'm not," I rasp.

"Take it up with Doc, not me. I'm just the messenger here for moral support for you or the staff, whoever needs it."

I smile because that's all I can do. I'm still tired, and my throat is killing me. "I'm going to close my eyes and sleep some of this soreness off. Why don't you go home and shower."

"I'm not leaving…"

Xavier continues to speak, but nothing he says makes sense as I slip out of consciousness back into a deep sleep.

Two days later and a lot of arguing later, I'm in the hospital physical therapy room, again. Michael is here waiting for me, a little more excited than usual.

"Today is the day, Joy girl; are you ready?" he yells across the room because why wouldn't he?

His enthusiasm pervades the room, and I can't help but feel hopeful and excited to be here. He must know something I don't. I can see it in his expression.

"Isn't it too soon? I yell back at him.

He ignores me… Shocker!

We start to warm up and I'm anxious; I can feel it pulsing through my body. I feel the stretch of my fresh stitches and fight the negative talk inside my head telling me there is no way in hell I can do this today.

"I feel like warming up today is going to be a waste of time; can we just get to it?" I ask. Telling Michael that trying something is a waste of time is enough to start World War Three.

"Are you serious?" he exclaims.

Here comes the lecture in three, two, one: "You have been comatose for two days in bed, and you think *just getting to it*' will do the trick." He waves his hands in the air. "Joy, your best friend has had a baby; another one got pregnant since the last time you walked, and you think we're just going to get to it without a proper stretch and warm-up?"

"Yes, today I think we need to just get to it," I argue.

He shakes his head like a disappointed parent.

"Let's start walking then," he says looking down at me as I continue to stretch. There's no hesitation in his voice, no more excitement, just pure determination.

I convince myself Michael only gives in to my request because he knows deep down that I've been warming for this moment for months now, but he's too stubborn to admit it.

At the hospital facility, we have access to more machines and contraptions. He fits me into something similar to a neck brace that paramedics use to stabilize someone after an accident, but it goes from my hips to my armpits. It feels similar to a corset. I'm wearing it to support my upper half so I can focus all my energy on my lower half. My abs are in the best shape of my life thanks to all the core exercises Michael makes me do, but I appreciate the assistance of all the equipment I can get my hands on.

"Okay," Michael says, rubbing his hands together as if trying to warm them on a cold winter day.

"Don't get disappointed if you don't get this today."

I interrupt him, "Don't puss out on me now, Michael. You just said today is the day, so today is the fucking day, got it," I say with so much intensity I surprise both of us.

"Okay, then, let's not waste any more time."

He pushes my chair over the parallel bars. He places me as close as my chair will allow, then moves between the two bars, readying himself to lift me out of my chair. I hold up a finger to stop him and place both hands on each bar. I also brace myself and give him a nod, alerting him it's okay to lift me out.

He takes me by the small of my waist and pulls me out of my chair. I balance my weight between the two bars and nod, letting Michael know I'm ready.

"When you're ready, try to take a step. I'm here to hold you upright if you get off balance or your arms tire."

I look over to my left, and Xavier is here videoing with his phone, which he gave up doing months ago. He gives me an excited "You got this" and thumbs-up from behind his phone, making me smile.

I take a minute to balance my body and quiet my mind. I'm not nervous or scared. Maybe I'm a little afraid of being disappointed in myself again, but I push all the noise out of my mind and focus. Focus on every feeling in my body. Michael's voice snaps me out of my trance.

"Are you ready, or do you want to sit down for a minute."

"I'm ready," I say, feeling my heart races with a blend of exhilaration and anxiety, and I'm sure I look more like a baby deer than a grown adult, but I take a step… by myself… with no help! I moved my legs without machines!

Michael screams excitedly, and Xavier jumps off the bench as if I single-handedly won the Super Bowl. But no one notices me lying on the floor in all their celebrating. Michael let go of me when he was screaming, and down I went. After a minute of celebration, Michael stands over me, smiling from ear to ear, and says, "I wish I were sorry for letting you crash, but I'm not. I've been waiting to see you move your legs for almost a year now, and I don't think I've ever been so happy for anything in my life."

"Can you help me up so we can do this again?" I plead with him from the dirty floor.

Before Michael can lift me, Xavier is there and bouncing up and down like a pogo stick. "Babe, you did it. You did it. You did it." Sounding like a broken record.

I interrupt all the excitement and say, "Okay, guys, let's make sure this isn't a fluke thing, and I'm going to be able to take another step. We have a lot of work to do before we can celebrate."

Xavier raises one hand to stop Michael from lifting me. He bends down, resting on his knees, hands splayed out on each side of me as I look at him hovering over me.

"Are you going to help me up or hang out on the floor with me?" I ask, a bit puzzled as to why he's joined me down here.

He leans in close, his breath warm against my ear, and

whispers, "This is the first step to the rest of our lives. This means we are getting married and you're walking down the aisle."

He tenderly kisses my head. In that moment, surrounded by love and promise, I feel the weight of his words sink in, and I know a new chapter of our lives is beginning.

Epilogue

"Joy, I'm home."

"I'm in here," I yell back to Xavier as I gracefully maneuver myself between our twin nine year olds fighting over something in the pantry that they definitely shouldn't be eating since I'm trying to cook dinner simultaneously as I referee.

"Dad!"

"Dad!" roars through the kitchen as the twins fight to see who can say Dad louder.

He picks them both up, one in each arm, and just like that, he's the hero. Our thirteen-year-old daughter walks down the stairs, and the twins immediately scream her name.

"How's my favorite daughter?" Xavier says.

Olivia rolls her eyes. "Hey, Dad," she says.

"Mom, can you take me to Aunt Roxy's? She's taking Kadin, Hazel, and me to the mall, and then we're having a sleepover at Aunt Harper's."

Kadin, Hazel, and Olivia. Roxanne gave birth to Kadin three months before Hazel and Olivia came eleven months later. They are all best friends. Kadin plays soccer like her mom, Hazel dances, and Olivia plays softball. All the different sports keep our three families busy and together every weekend.

Harper and I had a terrible start; two people who would've never been friends but were forced together by circumstance became family. Xavier showed us that there is beauty in everyone we meet. Something to love about everyone: I love Harper because she is honest. When I need to know if a dress makes my ass look fat, I go to her. She's taken me in and showed me more love than I ever experienced from my family.

I still haven't reconciled with my mom, nor do I have any plans to, but I have allowed her to see Olivia a few times over the years, and I keep her up to date on Olivia's adolescence through pictures. We help her when she needs it, and I text her to check on her well-being, which is more than she did for me growing up.

As far as my dad and his now almost adult children— We keep up with each other through social media. I throw away every Christmas card he sends and avoid them any time he or his wife tries to reach out. They are not my family. The three families I spend every weekend with watching our children grow up. That is my family. Harper's crazy family is my family now. Xavier's amazing mom is my mom now. Roxanne's family will always be my family. These people gave me something I didn't have growing up: a sense of belonging. We gave Harper something she never had growing up: confidence and self-love. We gave Roxanne something she never had growing up: a voice.

So, I will not allow my parents to control my feelings anymore; I reject the notion that I am unworthy of love, and I vow to shield my three children from ever experiencing even a fraction of the pain I endured in my own bringing.

"Earth to Mom," Olivia yells at me as she waves her hands in front of my face.

"Yes, I'll drive you to Kadin's, but why am I not invited to the mall?" I ask.

"Because you have the demon twins, and today is physical therapy day."

"Shoot," I exclaim. Looking at Xavier, I say, "That's why you're home early."

He nods as if he doesn't have a care in the world, still holding two very unruly twins on each hip.

It's been fifteen years since the accident and fourteen years since the day I retook my first steps. Xavier and I got married as soon as I was steady on my feet in a minimal ceremony. I walked down the aisle alone, surrounded by the silent support of Roxanne and Harper, my bridesmaids, whose tears spoke volumes of the depth of our shared journey.

I survived a near-fatal accident that, still, fifteen years later, makes zero sense to me. I was wheelchair-bound for one year, and the man of my dreams never left my side. He showed me that no matter the circumstance, he truly wanted me. I look around at my family, and a warm rush of validation and love fills my chest. The weight of lifelong doubt lifts, replaced by a profound sense of being cherished. The world righted itself the day I met him, and now I can breathe freely, knowing his feelings are unwavering, and we have our very own family to cherish always.

Coming Soon

from Kara Jefferies...

Harper and Joy:
THE FINAL CHAPTERS

KARA JEFFERIES

Release date: Fall 2024

EXCERPT

Chapter One

KADIN

High School Graduation

For the past four years, I woke up early and stayed up all night studying for finals, all leading to this moment. It felt like today would never happen, but I am, standing on the precipice of a new chapter. The past seemed like a relentless cycle of early mornings and sleepless nights, each day blending into the next with the singular purpose of reaching this milestone: graduation.

My phone buzzes on my vanity, pulling my attention from my mirror. Without looking down, I slid the notification and opened FaceTime.

"Are you riding with us?" Hazel, one of my best friends, asks as she makes an O with her mouth while putting on mascara in her vanity mirror.

"No, I told you already I'm riding with Jett." Jett and I live four houses apart from each other. He was my first friend outside of my parents' influence. Hazel and Olivia, I've known each other since birth, but Jett and I met while waiting at the bus stop on our first day of kindergarten, and we've been inseparable ever since.

"Kadin, it's our last day of high school; the three of us need to go together."

"Sorry." Not waiving from my convictions. Jett and I have walked onto the school campus together on the first and the last day of school since kindergarten, and today is no different. I'm going to change my mind. I'll see you and Olivia at our normal meeting spot."

"UGH!" she growls into the phone.

"Why aren't you driving with Hayes?"

"I am he's picking Olivia and me up. What is that supposed to mean anyway?" irritation laces her question.

"It just means we're finally out of high school, and maybe it's time you and Hayes stop playing games."

"I have go." That's all I get back as she blows me a kiss before hanging up on me. I stare at the blank screen, a smile tugging at my lips. Classic Hazel, always avoiding anything that has to do with Hayes Emmerson. I can't help but wonder if she'll admit just how much she's always loved him. They've been one of my best friends forever, and yet, here we all are, stuck in this weird limbo where they blissfully deny their feelings for each other.

There's a honk outside my house, and I run downstairs, jumping to the landing and skipping the last two stairs.

"You're going to break your damn ankle one day doing that, and you won't be able to play soccer." My mom scolds me. I love soccer, but I wonder if she loves it more than I do.

I kiss her on the cheek. "Last day, I'll see you when I get home."

"Remember, after graduation, we're all going to dinner together." When my mom says we're all going to dinner, that means Hazel and her parents, Olivia and her parents and twin brothers, my parents and four siblings, Jett and his parents, and Hayes's family. It's excessive with at least twenty people.

"Yeah, I know. The five of us are coming straight from

Graduation, so we'll meet you there."

"You're acting like I won't see you after graduation for pictures," I tease, rolling my eyes with a playful grin.

"Oh yeah, I guess I forgot that part," my mom says, a hint of nostalgia in her voice. "I gotta go, Mom. Jett is waiting."

She stands at the door, leaning against the frame, watching as I dash down the few steps of our walkway. Her eyes follow me, a mix of pride and bittersweet emotions flickering across her face. I jump into the passenger seat of Jett's car, feeling the familiar rush of excitement.

About Kara Jefferies

I write realistic Contemporary Romance novels with main characters you can't help but fall in love with and enough family drama to keep you reading.

When I'm not writing, you can find me with my husband chasing the sun on a beach somewhere. I was born and raised in Southern California but now live in Texas with our three dogs and daughter.

I'm an avid runner and love coffee and all things beauty.

Kara loves to hear from readers. You can find her contact information, website and author biography at **www.karajefferies.com**.

Also by Kara Jefferies

A Girl Named Harper

Harper and Joy: The Final Chapters